Change of Heart

Change of Heart

Dorothy P. O'Neill

AVALON BOOKS
THOMAS BOUREGY AND COMPANY, INC.
401 LAFAYETTE STREET
NEW YORK, NEW YORK 10003

PRINTED IN THE UNITED STATES OF AMERICA
ON ACID-FREE PAPER
BY HADDON CRAFTSMEN, SCRANTON, PENNSYLVANIA

Change of Heart

Chapter One

Deirdre Lane unlocked the door of her shop and flipped the sign to read OPEN.

A sudden breeze took hold of her hair and silky brown strands swirling over her face. Her denim skirt whipped around her slim legs.

A smile lighted her hazel eyes. There was a hint of autumn in that small puff of wind. She remembered last year when the end of the regular tourist season had brought a different kind of traveler to New Mexico—the sort who didn't haggle over prices or take half an hour deciding whether or not to buy a two-dollar souvenir.

Soon they'd be here again and if this fall were anything like the last, the shop would do a fair business through the Christmas season. These autumn tourists, along with local residents who did their Christmas shopping in Albuquerque's Old Town, would keep things going.

The shop was tucked away down a secluded, brick-paved walkway, its adobe walls blending into those of surrounding buildings. In one of its two small windows stood a display of Native American art—three Hopi kachina dolls, a Zuni bracelet, and a Navajo squash-blossom necklace. In the other was one of her sister Candace's hand-painted kachina shirts.

Above the door hung their sign, a piece of weathered barn siding with Indian symbols bordering the shop's name: *Kachinas and Things*.

Glancing up at it, Deirdre recalled how Candace had toiled to finish it in time for the shop's opening. She had sat in her wheelchair alongside her table of paints and materials, her golden-blond head bent over her work.

"Candy, let me find someone else to do it," Deirdre had said.

"We've dreamed for a long time about having a shop, and I want every bit of it to be ours," Candy had replied.

That had been more than a year ago. Soon after, Candy had started designing and painting the shirts and they had proved so popular that she seldom came into the shop anymore. To keep the shirts in stock and fill special orders, she worked at home in the studio their father had built for her when the shop was only a dream two sisters shared.

How proud he and Mother would have been of them. The thought brought Deirdre the familiar twinge of sadness, but no trace of the tears she'd shed for weeks after the car crash that had taken their lives and left Candy scarred, crippled, and subject to seizures. Deirdre's grief had begun to heal; her bitter heartache for Candy had not.

At first it was just a comfort to live in the house their father had designed especially for the mountainside he and Mother had loved. Now it was a joy. Deirdre found herself seeing everything through their eyes—moonlight on snowy slopes, the flash of a roadrunner's tail in the brush, piñons silhouetted against a lowering sun. . . .

This, and knowing Candy had accepted her personal tragedy and was making the best of life, eased Deirdre's bitterness but couldn't banish it completely. She only had to look into Candy's once-beautiful face, to remember Paul's cold, insensitive words and her own voice telling him their engagement was ended, to have the bitter disillusionment flood back.

A man's voice broke into her musing.

"Are you ready for the first of the big spenders?"

A lean, rangy figure was striding toward her. He was wearing blue jeans, a red-and-white checked shirt, and a Western-style hat under which several strands of sandy hair strayed over his brow.

Deirdre thought he might be handsome, if it weren't for the tired look on his face. His eyes were clouded with a weariness that made them seem more gray than blue.

"I'm ready—come on in," she said with a smile.

He followed her into the shop.

"Are you looking for anything in particular?" she asked.

His reply was quick and emphatic. "Yes. I want a kachina."

"You've come to the right place. We have a good selection. Is there one you're especially interested in?"

"Well, not really."

"Do you have a Butterfly in your collection?" she asked. "We have a fine one—and also a Mud Head by the same artist."

His blank expression told her he hadn't the slightest idea what she was talking about.

He spoke again with a sudden grin that briefly drove the tired look from his face and filled his eyes with a kind of roguish humor.

"Just what is a kachina, anyway?"

She burst into a laugh. "I'm sorry," she managed to say, "I thought you were a born-and-bred New Mexican."

Still smiling, he touched the wide brim of his hat.

"I guess this had you fooled. I bought it a few minutes ago in a shop across the plaza. I'm from New York. This is my first visit to Old Town."

That would explain his weary look, she thought. He was feeling the effects of the high altitude that most Easterners experienced. She turned to a nearby display shelf.

"These figurines, or dolls as they're called by Native Americans, are Hopi kachinas. They're carved by hand out of cottonwood root. There are hundreds of different characters representing plants, animals, birds—all kinds of things. Each one has a spiritual significance...."

She paused. Perhaps she should direct him to the book they had about kachinas, instead of going on like a museum tour guide.

He studied the array along the shelf.

"I like this fellow here," he said. "What's his name?"

"That's the Owl Dancer."

He ran his hand over the feathers, then nodded.

"I'll take him."

While she wrapped it, he strolled about the shop. It was obvious he was totally unfamiliar with American Indian crafts. She was puzzled. Why had he been so determined to buy a kachina when he didn't even know what they were?

She handed him the package with a smile.

"Thank you. I hope you enjoy your Owl Dancer."

He touched the brim of his hat in a farewell gesture, and then he was gone.

What a nice man, she thought. *And what a good start for the day's sales.*

Later, she realized it had been a very good start. A woman from Michigan bought a Zuni teardrop necklace; a couple from Tennessee purchased three Acoma pots and a small Navajo blanket. A number of Santo Domingo rings and other small silver and turquoise items also sold, and there were only two of Candy's shirts left in stock.

Candy laughed that night when Deirdre told her.

"Guess I'll have to start getting up earlier in the morning," she said. She had painted three shirts that day.

Deirdre felt a pang of concern. Was Candy working too hard? But the doctors had assured her that Candy's general health was good, and it wasn't as though she were left alone in the house all day. Their parent's longtime house-keeper, Yolanda, came in every morning and stayed till Deirdre got home.

Yolanda still treated them as though they were little girls. Under her watchful eye, Candy wouldn't forget to take her medication or become so engrossed in her painting that she would skip lunch or work too long without a break.

Now nearing fifty, Yolanda was a large, si-newy woman who'd been a strong swimmer since childhood. She had learned in the river that flowed past her native pueblo. She saw to it that Candy got her prescribed swims in the pool, even in winter, when a solar cover was erected. When Candy wheeled around the grounds and along the wooded trails in her mo-torized chair, Yolanda always went with her, accompanied by the family dog, Perro, whose lineage included a touch of coyote.

Their grandmother didn't approve of their life-style. She was constantly phoning and writing from Florida, insisting that Candy and Deirdre shouldn't be living in such a remote area. She reminded them how far away they were from their only remaining family, and urged them to give up the shop and move to Florida where she and Grandpa and Aunt Elizabeth could keep an eye on them.

It wasn't as if they needed the money, she would say when she called. It was ridiculous for Deirdre to slave in the shop and Candy to exhaust herself with all that painting. And in her last letter she'd told Deirdre about a good-looking young man Grandpa had met at the country club. He was a dentist and single. She'd underlined single—a not-so-subtle hint that it was time Deirdre started looking around for another possible fiancé.

"You're not getting any younger," she would say, as if twenty-four were over the hill. "But who knows, you might find another man like Paul."

Dear Grandmother, she meant well. But after the way all those guys who used to hang around Candy had disappeared and after what had happened with Paul, Deirdre's opinion of men's basic values had made her not only wary but disinterested.

She had put Paul out of her heart, but the reason for their parting had stayed in her mind. Anger and disillusionment had kept it there, perhaps to protect her from getting involved with any man, ever again.

It had happened on a delightful summer night, a few months after the accident. She and Paul were sitting on the patio near the pool. The dark-indigo sky was New Mexico clear, studded with a thousand stars. The air was heady with the scent of mountain pine and fir—a romantic setting that had made Paul's suggestion all the more repugnant.

When they'd become engaged, they'd planned to live in Paul's condo after getting married. The accident had changed that. Deirdre couldn't leave Candy.

"But there's loads of room for the three of us here," she'd told him, shortly after Candy came home from the hospital.

He had readily agreed.

But then, on that beautiful summer night, with their wedding only a few weeks away, he had told her that although he liked the idea of living in the Sandia foothills, he realized that Candy would be in a wheelchair and on medication for the rest of her life.

"I don't want us spending the rest of *our* lives taking care of her," he'd said.

Then he'd spoken the words that first had shattered her heart, then numbed it, then turned it to stone.

"We'll have to put her in a nursing home."

Deirdre hadn't told anyone why she'd broken the engagement. She wanted to make sure Candy would never know.

Now, Candy was wheeling around the kitchen, setting the table for their dinner, while Deirdre put Yolanda's chicken enchilada casserole into the microwave.

"So you had a good day at the shop," Candy said.

"One of the best. I'd only just opened when I sold the Owl Dancer to a nice man—a tourist from New York—and after that it was one sale after another all day long."

"Sounds like you could have used some help. I'll go in with you tomorrow in case it's another busy one. I'll bring my work. Maybe I can get a couple of shirts done in between customers."

Deirdre's heart brimmed anew with love and admiration for Candy. Disfigurement and infirmity had not clouded her sunny disposition nor crushed her indomitable spirit.

She pictured funny, lovable Candy shut away in a nursing facility, apart from everything she held dear. Again, her anger rose and she breathed the same promise she'd made on the night she'd sent Paul out of her life.

As long as I'm able, we'll be together, Candy. Nothing, no one, is going to put us apart.

* * *

The next morning, while Deirdre was arranging a tray of rings in the showcase, she looked up to see the New York tourist coming into the shop.

He was wearing jeans and a Western shirt again, and his eyes beneath his wide-brimmed hat looked as weary as they had yesterday.

"That's the man who bought the Owl kachina," she whispered to Candy.

Candy paused in her painting to peer over the countertop.

"You didn't tell me he was such a hunk," she whispered back.

Deirdre greeted him with a smile.

"Good morning. I hope everything's all right. I mean, are you satisfied with your kachina?"

"The Owl's fine," he said, smiling in return. "I had some spare time and decided to do some more shopping in Old Town."

His glance roved the shop and came to rest on Candy.

"What's that you're painting?" he asked.

"It's a Butterfly kachina shirt," Candy replied, holding it up for him to see.

He strode over for a closer look.

"Say, that's great."

"If you'd like one, I can paint you one with any kind of design you want on it," she said.

"Maybe you'd like an Owl Dancer to go with the kachina you bought yesterday."

Deirdre saw his eyes sweep over Candy's scarred face and linger briefly on the wheelchair, before he nodded and smiled.

"Yes, I'd like an Owl kachina shirt."

Candy reached for her order forms.

"Small, medium, large, or extra large?"

"Extra large. How soon can I have it?"

"It will be ready tomorrow afternoon."

"If you're leaving town, we can ship it to you," said Deirdre.

He cast her a puzzled look. "Leaving town?"

"Yes, didn't you say you were from New York?"

"I did, but I'm living out here now," he said.

He paid for the shirt and filled in his name and address on the order form. Deirdre noted that his name was G. R. Burns, and he lived in the university area of Albuquerque.

"Thank you, Mr. Burns." She extended her hand. "I'm Deirdre Lane and the artist is my sister, Candace."

"I'm Gordon," he said, and briefly clasped her hand.

At that moment Deirdre saw the pastor of their church coming into the shop. She and Candy had known Mr. Gillespie since their Sun-day-school days. Seeing him reminded her that they hadn't been attending church as often as they had before opening the shop.

"It's good to see you, Mr. Gillespie," she said.

"It's good to see you too, ladies," he replied. "We've missed you. I guess the shop keeps you busy."

"Yes. It's difficult getting to services with the shop open on Sundays."

"I understand. I didn't come here to chide you. I want to talk to you, Deirdre, about a volunteer program the church is sponsoring at the prison. It would only take half an hour of your time every week, and you could choose the time."

During this exchange, Deirdre was aware of Gordon Burns listening with obvious interest.

"I hate to say no, Mr. Gillespie, but I'd find it just as difficult to spare half an hour for volunteer work as I would finding time for church."

"Let me tell you more about it," the minister said. "It involves talking to an individual inmate at the prison. There are certain men in there who haven't had a visitor since they were locked up. This is an experimental program designed to make them feel they haven't been totally rejected by society. The prison psychiatrist feels it will be of help in their rehabilitation."

"Do you think I'd be any good at this?" she asked.

"I've known you most of your life, Deirdre, and I know you have the qualities needed for this kind of program. If once a week would be too much for you, maybe you'd consider every two weeks. Please think about it."

What loneliness and despair a man must feel if no one came to visit during his incarceration, Deirdre thought.

"How long would the program run?" she asked.

"As I said, it's experimental. You can stop any time you want. The psychiatrist feels all avenues must be explored towards the rehabilitation of these men."

"Do it, Dee Dee," Candy said. "I can cover the shop, and if it gets too busy I can call Yolanda to help."

Deirdre hesitated for a moment before acquiescing. "All right, Mr. Gillespie. And as long as I'm going to do it, I might as well go every week."

The minister smiled broadly.

"I knew I could count on you, Deirdre. I'll let you know the details in a day or so."

After he left, Deirdre turned to Candy with a wry smile. "You had to open your big mouth, didn't you?"

"Don't blame me," Candy said. "I could tell you were interested. Anyway, you need something in your life besides looking after me and working here."

They had both forgotten that Gordon Burns was still there. Now they heard his voice from the other side of the shop.

"It sounds like you're in for some challenging sessions, Deirdre. I worked in a penitentiary for a while, back East. It can be quite interesting."

He headed for the door and cast a smile over his shoulder.

"I'll be in to pick up the shirt tomorrow, Candace."

They watched him stride down the walkway.

"He likes you, Dee Dee," Candy said. "I saw the way he looked at you."

"He was only being pleasant."

"Well, when he comes in tomorrow, you be pleasant too."

"You know I'm always nice to the customers."

"That's not what I mean and you know it!"

Deirdre did know. Since her breakup with Paul, she'd had only a few casual dates. Candy thought it was time she developed a serious relationship.

"Candy, you're getting more like Grandmother every day," she said. "We don't know anything about this Gordon Burns. He could be married."

"He wasn't wearing a wedding ring."

"Not all men do."

"Well, tomorrow we can ask him some subtle questions, like 'is this shirt for your wife?'" Candy paused, chuckling. "But that's not likely—he ordered size extra large."

"Maybe she's pregnant."

"You just won't get into the spirit of this, will you?" Candy sighed.

"I'll go as far as admitting I think he's nice. But we can't even be sure of that. How about that remark he made about working in a prison? Maybe he was really a convict."

The appearance of several customers put an end to the discussion. When the shop was empty again, Deirdre thought about the prison program for which she'd volunteered.

What had she gotten herself into? What sort of man would she be talking to for half an hour every week? What crime had he committed and how long had he been in prison? There must be some good reason why no one had visited him all that time. He was probably such a slimy character that even his own mother had given up on him.

Candy's voice broke into her thoughts. "You're

awfully quiet, Dee Dee. I'll bet you were think-ing about that nice Gordon Burns."

"Wrong. I was wondering why I got involved in that prison program."

"You're not going to back out, are you?"

"No, I couldn't let Mr. Gillespie down after I said I'd do it."

"I wish I could do it," Candy said, "but I know why Mr. Gillespie didn't ask me."

She ran her fingers over her cheeks and nose. "Until I have some more plastic surgery on my face, I'd be known to the prisoners as 'Scarface Blondie.'"

What a rare sense of humor Candy had. Even while she was laughing, Deirdre was thinking how ironic it was that, despite being disabled and disfigured, Candy was the one without bit-terness.

She found herself hoping, praying, that the next facial surgery, scheduled for November, would restore some of Candy's former good looks.

Candy had started painting the Owl shirt for Gordon Burns.

"I want this to be especially good," she said. "I want to keep that man coming into the shop."

Deirdre couldn't help thinking that Gordon Burns would be back in the shop again and again if Candy still looked the way she had before the accident. Candy had been prettier than Deirdre. Grandmother was right; men did go for pretty faces.

Deirdre wondered about handsome Paul Martin. Had he really loved her? He was just out of architectural school when they met, and her father was one of Albuquerque's leading architects. Had Paul's attraction to her been largely career-motivated? And after her father died, was Paul drawn to her because she had a beautiful home in the Sandias and the means to maintain it?

Candy was holding up the Owl shirt. "How do you like it so far?" There was no doubt she was taking special pains with it.

"It's going to be beautiful," Deirdre said. "Just wait till you see the look on Gordon Burns's face when he comes in to pick it up tomorrow."

"I'm staying home tomorrow," Candy replied. "You'll have to get his reaction all by yourself!"

Chapter Two

"Say, this turned out great! Be sure and tell your sister how pleased I am with it," Gordon Burns said. He was examining the shirt, and Deirdre noticed that although his hands looked strong and capable, he handled the painted fabric with surprising gentleness.

"I'm sorry she didn't come in today so you could tell her yourself," Deirdre replied. Her efforts to get Candy to come with her had only resulted in teasing remarks.

"That man will be more likely to ask you for a date if I'm not there," Candy had said.

Deirdre thrust this possibility from her mind.

"If there's nothing else that catches your eye, I'll wrap up the shirt," she said.

Gordon hesitated before replying. "Well, there *is* something else. Would you consider having dinner with me this evening?"

Taken by surprise, she didn't know what to say. Half of her brain began sending out warning signals that she didn't know the first thing about this man or his motives, while the other half was telling her he was just a stranger in a strange town who didn't want to eat another dinner alone.

He was looking at her intently.

"I understand your reluctance. For all you know about me, I could be Jack the Ripper."

She laughed, then asked herself what harm there would be in a casual dinner. After she closed the shop, they could walk to one of the nearby restaurants. Afterward, they'd go their separate ways.

"I'd be delighted to have dinner with you tonight," she said. A moment later she began to feel apprehensive, but it was too late. He was asking her what time she closed the shop and telling her he'd be back to take her to dinner.

The restaurant was in a restored adobe house, once the residence of a wealthy landowner in the days when old Mexico's boundaries extended from the Pacific Ocean to the Rocky Mountains.

Deirdre could see that Gordon was fascinated

with the rough-hewn vigas across the ceilings, the well-worn Mexican brick flooring, and the curving walls with windowlike openings between the rooms.

"Are there many old houses like this still standing in New Mexico?" he asked.

"Oh, yes—especially in Santa Fe."

"I haven't had time to see Santa Fe yet," he said. "Maybe we could drive up there someday and you could show me around."

While she was trying to decide how to answer, he was glancing at the menu and asking her to help him order.

"I haven't been out here long enough to learn much about real Southwestern food," he said. "All I'm familiar with is the New York version of chile con carne."

She made some suggestions, making sure he wouldn't be confronted with a plateful of food too spicy for his Eastern palate.

When they were served, he looked across the table at her and smiled.

"Thanks for coming out with me, Deirdre."

"Thanks for asking me. I take it you don't know anyone in Albuquerque."

"I know a few people. I hope you didn't think I asked you to have dinner with me because there was no one else."

He seemed to read her mind. Why had he asked her?

"When I saw you outside your shop that morning, I wanted to get to know you," he said. "I noticed your shop sign and decided the quickest way would be to barge right in and tell you I wanted to buy a kachina."

"Even though you didn't know what a kachina was!" She laughed. "You were taking an awful chance. You could have found yourself the proud owner of a chief's warbonnet!"

He studied her face. "You were smiling like that when I saw you outside your shop," he said. "You have a million-dollar smile, Deirdre."

She thanked him for the compliment. She could imagine Candy saying, "I *told* you he liked you."

"How long have you and your sister worked in the shop?" Gordon asked.

"More than a year. But we don't just work there. The shop is ours."

"Your own business—that's great," he said. He paused, the trace of a frown crossing his face. "Would I be out of line if I asked what happened to your sister?"

"Not at all," she replied. She told him about the accident.

He shook his head. "What a tragedy. I can't

even imagine how hard it must have been for you both."

"With all her suffering, Candy has taken it better than I. Losing our parents was a terrible blow, but she's been through so much more. She's had two facial surgeries, and she's having another soon. The doctors say her looks can be improved, but she'll never be able to walk again. She has another problem too, but that's being controlled by medication."

Her words were spilling out in a torrent, as though they'd been dammed up in her mind by sorrow and heartache.

"I assume she's been examined by more than one specialist," he said.

"Three. They all said the same thing. There's no operation that could bring back the use of her legs."

"Did they give you any hope about the seizures?"

She looked at him in surprise. How did he know that this was Candy's other problem?

He must have seen the question in her eyes.

"I'm a doctor, Deirdre. I've seen a lot of people messed up in accidents."

"You're a doctor?" She stared at him for a moment, then started to laugh. "After you told us you'd worked in a prison, I warned Candy that you might actually have been an inmate."

He joined in with a chuckle. "And yet you came with me anyway. You must have considered me thoroughly reformed."

From that moment on, the apprehension she had felt eased, then disappeared. They asked questions and talked, asked more questions and talked some more, until she found herself feeling she'd known Gordon for years instead of days.

He didn't have to tell her he wasn't married. That he was single was evident in his description of his family and his life in the New York suburbs where his father was an attorney and his mother managed a fashion boutique. One of his sisters was married, he told her; the other was in college. Deirdre had a distinct impression of a warm, close family.

It was while he was in medical school in New York that he'd worked for a short time in a state prison. Now he was a resident physician at the University of New Mexico hospital and was presently assigned to emergency-room duty on the late shift.

"I haven't had much sleep since I've been here," he said.

Now she knew why he looked tired. She pictured him on duty, his strong, gentle hands ministering to the needs of people sick or injured, frightened and in pain.

She told him about Yolanda and Perro, about

the house in the Sandia foothills, and about the ever-changing enchantment of the mountainside.

She found herself wanting him to experience it all, to walk along the wooded trails and see jackrabbits and roadrunners scurrying across his path, to watch the western sky turn to coral and gold above the treetops, hear the wind sweeping down the wooded slopes, breathe its piney scent, and feel its touch upon his face.

Hold it, came a warning from the recesses of her mind. *It's all right to enjoy a meal and conversation with this man, but you'd be asking for trouble if you invited him out to the house.*

She knew the kind of trouble it would be. She already liked him too much. Letting him share what she held dear would risk opening up her heart again.

Through her reverie she heard his voice.

"When are you going to start your prison visits?"

She was glad of the chance to turn her mind away from those disturbing thoughts.

"I don't know yet. The minister's going to phone me about it."

"I'd be interested to know how it goes. Would you mind if I dropped in at the shop once in a while? I might even buy something."

It sounded so harmless, but she sensed the danger lurking behind his words.

"Drop in anytime," she said, hoping her voice sounded as impersonal as she was trying to make it. "You're always welcome, whether you buy anything or not."

She glanced at her watch.

"I should be going. Yolanda's staying with Candy and I don't like to keep her there too long."

He walked her to her car in the shadowy parking lot.

"Aren't you ever nervous, driving out to the mountains after dark?" he asked.

"I've done it so often, I could almost drive the roads blindfolded. I know every bump and turn."

She extended her hand. "Gordon, thank you. I enjoyed it."

"I did too." He clasped her hand briefly. "I'll see you soon in the shop. Say hello to Candy for me."

She drove homeward through the deepening dusk with her mind in a turmoil. She kept remembering what he'd said about her smile. There was no doubt he wanted to see her again—and not just in the shop. What harm would there possibly be in having dinner with him again—or even driving up to Santa Fe with him sometime?

By the time she turned the car off the highway onto the dirt road which led up toward the house, she was almost angry. Why was her mind spinning these thoughts when she had no heart for them?

The sound of her key in the door brought Perro bounding to greet her. Deirdre gave his scruffy head a few strokes before going into the den where Candy and Yolanda were watching television.

Candy's face was alight with curiosity and her voice just as excited as it had been when she heard that Deirdre was having dinner with Gordon.

"How did it go?" she asked.

Apparently she'd briefed Yolanda. The two of them were staring, as though Deirdre were Cinderella back from the ball.

She told them where they'd had dinner and what she'd learned about Gordon.

"So he's a doctor; that's good," Yolanda said, nodding approval. Her curiosity satisfied, she went home.

"You did enjoy yourself, didn't you?" Candy asked.

"Yes, it was very pleasant. He's a nice man."

"Are you going to see him again?"

"Well, he said he'd drop in at the shop sometime."

Candy sighed. "You didn't give him any encouragement at all, did you?"

Suddenly she sat upright in her chair.

"Oh, Dee Dee, I almost forgot—Mr. Gillespie phoned and wants you to call him back tonight."

Deirdre was glad to change the subject. She immediately returned the minister's call and was told the visiting program at the prison was to begin the following week. She decided on her time slot and was given instructions.

"Do you know anything about the man I've been assigned to talk with?" she asked Mr. Gillespie.

"His name is Herman. He's a young fellow who has been imprisoned for about six months. I wasn't told what he'd been convicted of, but don't be nervous, Deirdre. The warden assured me that the men chosen for the program aren't considered dangerous."

She wasn't at all nervous. She was eager to start. With her mind channeled in this new direction, she wouldn't be thinking about Gordon.

The young inmate stared at Deirdre across the table. There was hostility in his eyes and in the grudging way he slumped his stocky frame into his chair without any sign of greeting. His hair fell in straggles about his neck and strayed in dark wisps above the contours of a face not fully hardened.

He's scarcely more than a boy, she thought.

"Hello," she said. "My name is Deirdre Lane. I'll be coming to visit you every week."

"Yeah, they told me," he replied with a shrug. As he spoke, he didn't look directly at Deirdre, but fastened his gaze somewhere beyond her.

"Your name is Herman, isn't it?"

His dark eyes held a sullen look.

"You didn't have to ask me. They already told you that and everything else about me," he said.

"It's true I was told your name, but other than that I know nothing about you," she said. "I was hoping you'd tell me yourself."

"You want to know how many people I've killed?" he asked with a sneer.

She took a deep breath, trying to quell an impulse to turn around and leave this young punk to stew in his own hostility. Mr. Gillespie had said he wasn't considered dangerous, but he had a bad attitude. He seemed to resent her being there.

She decided to give it a few more minutes. Managing a smile, she tried again.

"I thought we could talk about where we grew up—our families and—"

"I got no family."

"I have no mother or father either. They died

in an automobile accident. But I do have a sister. We live together."

She thought she saw a flicker of response in his eyes, but he made no reply.

"I have a dog too," she went on. "His name is Perro. He's part coyote. Did you ever have a dog, Herman?"

He shook his head.

This visit was going nowhere, she thought. She wanted to leave. She glanced around the room. Other inmates were deep in conversation with their visitors. Was she the only one who'd come as a volunteer? Holding back a sigh, she made another attempt to draw him into conversation.

"I was born and raised in Albuquerque," she said. "Where did you grow up, Herman?"

For a moment she thought he was going to ignore her question. Then he answered, still not meeting her eyes.

"I'm from Albuquerque too."

It was a start, she thought.

"What part of Albuquerque did you live in?"

"Near Old Town,"

"My sister and I have a shop in Old Town. We sell Indian artwork and jewelry, and my sister paints shirts with Indian designs."

He slouched back in his chair, still averting his eyes from hers. She could think of nothing else to talk about and the silence between them was as much a barrier as the glass stretched across the table.

She glanced at her watch. A scant fifteen minutes had passed. She decided it was useless to continue the visit.

"I'm going now," she said. She wasn't surprised when he made no reply.

She hesitated. If he'd only give some sign that he wasn't totally averse to her visit, perhaps she'd stay. But he was already getting up to leave.

"I'll come again next week," she said.

He shrugged. "Suit yourself."

Then he turned his back and signaled the guard that the visit was over.

Back in Old Town, Deirdre entered the walkway and paused to call through the open doorway of the shop next door. She always alerted a neighbor when Candy was alone.

"Ralph—I'm here."

His portly frame loomed in the entrance.

"It's been a quiet morning," he told her. "A few Indians came around selling jewelry and two ladies were here, then went to your place. Candy must have sold something—I saw them leaving with bags."

"Well, at least it won't be one of those zero days," Deirdre said.

"There's a man in your shop now," Ralph added. "I was just about to stick my head in and check. He looked okay, though. I think he's been around here before. Tall fellow—wears a Western hat."

"Thanks, Ralph," Deirdre said, above the sudden pounding of her heart.

Gordon was studying a tray of rings and Candy was getting another tray out of the showcase. They both looked up when Deirdre entered, Candy with a knowing grin, Gordon with a warm smile.

"Hi, Deirdre, Candy told me you've started your prison visits," he said.

"Hello, Gordon. Yes, the program began today."

She turned to Candy. "Ralph says it's been a slow morning."

"Not any more," Candy said. "Gordon's picking out rings for his mother and sisters."

Deirdre went into the back room and hung up her purse and sweater. She knew that most visitors to Old Town made the rounds of the shops and the sidewalk vendors before deciding what to buy. Yet Gordon was doing all his buying here.

Candy's comment came back to her. "He likes you, Dee Dee."

She drew a deep breath and joined Candy behind the counter, watching Gordon's hands move almost caressingly over the rows of turquoise and silver rings.

"If you don't see anything you like, you might try the shop across the way," she said, ignoring Candy's frown.

He cast her a quizzical glance.

"I've found what I want, right here."

Something in his eyes made her heart skip a beat.

"I'll take this green one for my mother and the two blue ones for my sisters," he said.

While Candy rang up the sale, he moved down the counter opposite Deirdre.

"How did your prison visit go?" he asked.

"It wasn't what you'd call a howling success. I'm not looking forward to the next one."

"I take it the inmate wasn't receptive."

She laughed. "You could certainly say that!"

"I'd like to hear more about it sometime."

She knew he was going to ask her for a date. A glance at Candy told her Candy knew it too. She was trying to suppress a knowing grin.

"A few of us from the hospital are getting together Saturday at the home of two of the residents. They said for me to bring someone if I wanted to. How about going with me, Deirdre?"

An excuse for turning him down immediately came to mind. Yolanda had a family gathering scheduled for that night.

But before Deirdre could speak, Candy was interrupting.

"I know what you're going to say, Dee Dee, and I wish you'd get it out of your head once and for all that I need a baby-sitter."

"I don't like the idea of your being alone, especially at night," Deirdre replied. She turned to Gordon. "Thanks for asking me, anyway."

Candy frowned. "Please go, Dee Dee. I'll be fine."

"You know how difficult it is for you to get to bed."

"You could get me settled in bed before you left," Candy insisted.

Gordon had been listening to this exchange, looking from one to the other.

"I've just thought of something," he said. "Why don't you come along with us, Candy?"

Candy looked at him. Her hands went to her face, traveling the length of her scars.

"It'll be okay," Gordon said. "There will be mostly doctors there—some married, some not. Those who have kids will bring them. All very casual. And I promise to have you home early. I have to be on duty at midnight."

Candy glanced at Deirdre. "If there's no other way you'll agree, Dee Dee—"

It was plain, Candy wanted to go. Deirdre nodded. "All right, Gordon, you've got yourself two dates for Saturday night."

"Great," he said. "I'll pick you up around seven. How do I get out to your place?"

"We could meet you at the party," she suggested. "That way you wouldn't have to drive way out to the foothills."

"No way," he said. "I'm old-fashioned. I like to call for my dates and see them home."

Candy's eyes were shining. "It's been a long time since either of us has gone to a party," she said.

She was right, Deirdre thought. Except for occasional visits with friends or neighbors, Candy's social life had ended with the accident, and her own had dwindled after her breakup with Paul.

She gave Gordon directions and sketched a crude map.

"I won't have any trouble finding it, I'm sure," he said.

He turned to Candy and said good-bye. Deirdre walked to the door with him. When they stepped outside, she told him she was concerned about the reception Candy would get at the party.

"I wouldn't have asked her to come along if I didn't know it would be all right," he said.

She knew he meant there'd be mostly doctors there. But he'd also mentioned children.

As though he'd read her thoughts, he added, "We both know Candy wouldn't be sensitive to anything a little kid might say about her face."

It was true. Whatever hurt Candy had sustained since her disfigurement had come from those whose years should have given them tact and understanding.

She watched him walk away. Just before he rounded the corner, he turned with a smile and an upward thrust to the broad-brimmed hat she always associated with him.

There was a sudden softening of the rock-hard conviction she'd held for so long. There *could* be a difference. One man couldn't see beyond Candy's wheelchair and her scars; another could look straight into her face and ask her to go to a party.

But was Gordon as empathetic as he seemed? Maybe he hadn't had time to meet anyone else. He wanted someone to date now and then, and

if that couldn't be accomplished without sometimes including a disabled sister. . . .

Before she went back into the shop, she'd almost convinced herself of this.

Almost.

Chapter Three

Whatever misgivings Deirdre had, they soon vanished after the door to the small house on Amherst Street was swung open by a young woman with a round, pleasant face. She was joined by a tall, slightly balding young man carrying a little boy.

"Hello, Gordon," the man said. He smiled at Deirdre and Candy. "I'm Jake Miller and this is our younger son, Sam."

"And I'm Amy. Come on in," the woman added.

"So you're the Old Town sisters Gordon keeps talking about," Jake said. He helped Gordon get Candy's chair through the doorway.

Amy laughed. "Gordon's some kind of fast

worker, isn't he? In town only a couple of months and showing up here with not just one, but two dates!"

The small, sparsely furnished living room was filled with people, most of them sitting on the floor, and with the sound of long-ago big band music—Benny Goodman, Deirdre guessed.

Everyone looked up with a warm greeting as Jake made general introductions. He and Gordon settled Candy's chair into a corner not too close to the sound system and out of the way of those who couldn't resist dancing to the infectious rhythms.

"We don't want you losing your hearing when the brass section comes in," Gordon said, "or having some jitterbug land in your lap."

"I'll be fine here," Candy said. She glanced at the dancers, then at Deirdre. "Now, don't hover. Go and show me how it was done in Grandma's day."

Gordon looked at Deirdre.

"You heard the boss. Shall we?"

She nodded. His arm closed around her shoulders, his hand clasped hers, and she felt herself caught up in the swinging tempo. There was something wonderful in this old music, she thought—something she'd never heard at a rock concert.

She looked up into his eyes.

"You're a very good dancer, Gordon."

"Thanks. If I am, my older sister's responsible. We wore out a section of the living-room rug before I got the hang of it. You're very light on your feet yourself."

He looked around the crowded room with a wry smile.

"I can't fully demonstrate my terpsichorean talent tonight. Maybe sometime soon we could go someplace where we could really dance."

Before she could decide how to answer, Amy announced that the food was on the kitchen table and they were to help themselves.

When Deirdre saw the array of salads and casseroles on the table, she knew right away this was a potluck supper.

"I wish I'd known it was to be cooperative. I would have brought something," she told Amy.

"There's more than enough—we're just glad you came," Amy said.

Gordon was looking teasingly at Deirdre.

"You can cook too?"

"I'm a fair cook. But what do you mean, *too?*"

"I mean, in addition to your other fine attributes."

"And what might those be?"

She was enjoying the banter. She'd never felt so at ease with a man.

"Well," he said, "for one thing, you must have

good business sense to run your shop, and for another you must have self-confidence and compassion to take on that prison program. But most of all, your devotion to Candy tells me your sense of commitment is unwavering."

His last words touched her heart. She tried to hide a sudden rush of emotion with a laughing reply.

"Unwavering commitment! That sounds like a faithful dog!"

He scooped a portion of potato salad onto her plate and another onto his, then turned and looked straight into her eyes.

"Don't knock commitment, Deirdre."

A sense of words unspoken seemed to hang between them. Hastily, she sought to dispel it.

"I'll fill a plate for Candy," she said.

They looked over to where Candy was sitting. Someone had already taken a plate of food to her and several people had seated themselves on the floor near her wheelchair and were talking with her.

"You have nice friends, Gordon," Deirdre said.

"Yes, they're a good bunch," he agreed.

"Did you know any of them before you came out here? It seems like you're all quite close."

"Most of us were total strangers. I guess the rigors of being fellow residents drew us together very quickly, not to mention the biggest common bond of all—poverty!"

Deirdre looked around the sparsely furnished room.

"How do Amy and Jake manage, with two children?"

"I don't know, but their present situation is better than it was a year ago. They were married in medical school and both kids were born before graduation. Like many of us, they were living on student loans. Now, of course, they're getting salaries, but it's still not easy."

"Do many medical students marry while they're in school?"

"Sure. And a lot of them marry other medical students."

The question in her mind was spoken before she could hold back the words.

"How come you didn't marry while you were a medical student?"

"It's a long story," he said. He looked around the room. "Let's sit down over there and I'll tell you all about it."

An agitated voice within her told her this would be a big mistake. Knowing this personal part of his life would only draw her closer to him. She shouldn't let him confide in her.

But another voice told her there'd be no harm

in listening. It was as if her mind were divided—
or was it her heart?

Again she heard the first voice, telling her
that each new thing she learned about him was
another part added to a foundation upon which
she would never want to build.

But now it was too late. They were seated and
he was answering the question she'd so foolishly
asked.

"There was a woman I met while I was in
medical school. Her father's a prominent New
York surgeon—big, fancy office, elegant Manhattan apartment, a summer home on the Con-
necticut shore...." He paused. "We got pretty
serious, to the point where her father was already talking about me going into practice with
him after my residency, then taking over after
he retired. Sounds like a young doctor's dream
come true, doesn't it?"

"But it wasn't your own dream?"

"No. I had my own ideas about the kind of
practice I wanted. That's the reason I chose New
Mexico for my residency. I wanted to familiarize
myself with the Native American population. I
intend to set up my practice here, and to devote
part of it to improving Indian health care."

He glanced at Deirdre with the trace of a
forced smile.

"When I told Pamela, she dumped me."

Deirdre searched his eyes for the pain she hadn't heard in his voice. He seemed to know what she was seeking.

"Yes, it hurt for a while," he said, "but I know now it was the best thing that could have happened. Not only was her father's practice all wrong for me, but so was she."

Deirdre turned her eyes away from his, unwilling to see what might lie within them, yet hoping with all her heart it was there.

What am I afraid of, she asked herself, and the answer came without pause. Without actually announcing it, Gordon was being as straightforward as a man could be about his feelings for her. Those feelings had reached a plateau; now they were poised to scale new heights.

How skillfully he'd drawn her with him to this pinnacle. There was no turning back now from their deepening feelings, yet there was no ignoring the warning voice she kept hearing in her mind.

Gordon was being very kind to Candy. Was it the means to an end? If she didn't heed the warning, in the weeks and months to come would she hear those shattering words of a bygone starry night? She knew if she heard them from Gordon, she couldn't bear it. Better never to topple the fragile barrier between friendship and love.

The sound of his voice came into her thoughts.

"It looks like Candy's finished eating. Shall we see if she needs anything more?"

Deirdre suppressed a sigh. He couldn't know how his words reinforced her misgivings.

By the time they reached Candy's side, someone had already brought her a cup of coffee.

"You're being well taken care of, I see," Gordon said.

Candy nodded. "Indeed I am. This is a great party, isn't it? I watched you two dancing before. You looked like you'd waltzed right out of an old TV movie."

"Gordon's a regular Fred Astaire," Deirdre said. "I thought any minute we'd be dancing over tabletops."

She was glad of the chance to joke, to be free of her disturbing thoughts.

"Why don't you dance some more?" Candy asked. "That music is wonderful. Someone told me that's Glenn Miller playing now."

Gordon held out his arms to Deirdre.

"Shall we try for the tabletops?"

Over his shoulder, Deirdre saw Candy grin and give the thumbs-up sign.

Dancing is an unmistakable prelude to an embrace, Deirdre thought. The music and the footwork keep things on another level, but when the music stops you have only to linger an extra moment in your partner's encircling arm and keep your hand in his. . . .

Suddenly she realized the music *had* stopped and she *hadn't* stepped away from Gordon. His hand was still clasping hers and he was looking down at her, his eyes telling her that if they weren't in a room filled with people, he'd be kissing her.

She managed to get through the remainder of the evening without putting her heart at further risk. She avoided dancing with Gordon again. Instead, she went with Amy into the children's bedroom and watched two little boys saying their prayers and being tucked in for the night.

She mingled with Gordon's friends, asking them about their geographical roots and the medical schools they'd come from and what kind of practices they hoped to set up.

She danced with redheaded Will from Oregon, with dark, curly-haired Lionel from New Jersey, and with short, stocky Henry who wasn't a doctor but whose wife was, and whose very young baby was asleep in a bureau drawer in Amy and Jake's bedroom.

If Gordon noticed she was avoiding him, he gave no sign of it. She had joined a group gathered around Candy when he approached them with a rueful smile.

"I hate to break this up, but it's time we were leaving."

Deirdre remembered he had to be on duty at midnight. A glance at her watch told her there would be no time for him to stay a while after he'd taken them home. That was fine. No time for them to linger in the doorway, no risk of the kiss she knew would sweep away the barriers she'd been so carefully maintaining.

On the ride back to the foothills, she was grateful for Candy's animated talk.

"Thanks so much for taking me along tonight. I had a wonderful time. I'd like us to have a party, Dee Dee, and invite all those nice people who were there tonight. Maybe when things get slow at the shop, after Christmas. Maybe a New Year's party. What do you think, Dee Dee? Gordon?"

"Sounds good to me," Gordon said.

Deirdre thought about the big snowstorm that usually hit Albuquerque after Christmas. Didn't Candy remember last year when the highway east of the Sandias was almost impassable? The road up the mountainside to their driveway was blocked, and Yolanda's brother had to come out with a plow on his jeep and dig them out. If the storm hit the day before the party, there'd be no party. But worse, suppose it came *during* the party?

She imagined a houseful of guests unable to leave the mountainside. Candy must have given some thought to this herself. She was chuckling.

"I know what you're thinking, Dee Dee—the big Christmas storm could blow in right in the middle of the party. We'd all be snowed in!"

It was clear that Candy thought this would be a lark.

Gordon was turning the car onto the steep slope leading to the house.

"I can see where it wouldn't be easy to get up here in heavy snow," he said. "I'll bet you've been stranded more than once."

"We have," Deirdre replied. "But we always keep plenty of provisions on hand."

"We could feed a dozen people for a week," Candy boasted.

When they'd reached the house, Gordon lifted Candy's chair out of the car, unfolded it, and took it to the door. Deirdre unlocked the door and wheeled it in, while Gordon went back for Candy. He carried her into the house and seated her.

Deirdre had been right about the time factor. Gordon could only take a few moments to say good-bye. Deirdre saw him to the door.

Now would be the time for her to discourage him, she thought. But before she could put thought into words, she felt the fleeting touch of his hand upon her face. Then, with a final "good night," he was gone.

She stood in the open doorway and watched him drive off, her fingers tracing the place on her cheek where his hand had rested so briefly. The crunch of car tires on gravel grew faint, then disappeared into the quiet of the mountainside, before she turned and went inside.

"It's strange we haven't heard from Gordon since the party," Candy said.

She and Deirdre were in the shop the next week, and Deirdre was about to leave for her prison visit.

She didn't need to be reminded that Gordon hadn't called or dropped by. Every time the shop door opened, every time the phone rang that week, she'd felt her heart race. She was glad she was going to the prison today. Though she hadn't much hope that this second visit with Herman would be any better, at least she'd have something else to occupy her mind.

"Well, I'm ready to confront Mr. Congeniality again," she told Candy. "I'll tell Ralph you're here alone."

Candy grimaced. "Even if Ralph came in here and found some creep robbing us blind, what do you think he could do about it?"

They both laughed at the idea of paunchy, out-of-shape Ralph overpowering a thief of any age or condition.

"It's just that you look so vulnerable," Deirdre said.

"The wheels, you mean." Candy gave a sigh. "I suppose I do. We really should bring Daddy's hunting rifle into the shop. I could prop it up right here beside me." She chuckled. "I wouldn't look so helpless then, would I?"

Deirdre shook her head. Candy had suggested this before.

"The best place for Daddy's rifle is where it's always been—in the rack over the fireplace," she said firmly.

She headed for the door. "I'm off now. Be sure and sell lots of stuff."

Deirdre looked into Herman's sullen face again and asked herself why she'd bothered to come. The hostility in his eyes was as great as it had been the week before.

"How are you today, Herman?" she asked, knowing the question was inane, but she had to get the talk going somehow.

She wasn't surprised to be answered with a shrug. But an instant later, he spoke.

"I didn't think you'd come back."

"I said I would, didn't I?"

"Yeah, but people are always saying what they don't mean."

A flash of insight told her his life had been filled with broken promises.

"Perhaps," she said, "but I'm one of those who tries to live up to what I say."

Unlike the previous week, when he'd constantly glanced away, he was now looking directly at her. She saw a trace of puzzlement in his eyes.

"I really didn't want to come back," she said. "You know why, don't you, Herman?"

He stared at her for a moment. "Yeah. It was me making like I'd just as soon you didn't."

"That's right. But I'm here anyway, and I hope we can have a better visit today."

This time his answering shrug did not seem as hostile.

"Tell me about yourself," she said. "What are you interested in? Do you like sports? Do you watch the ball games on TV?"

His eyes brightened. "Yeah. Baseball."

She knew enough about baseball to make a few comments about the leagues. He began to talk and she learned which team he was rooting for and the names of players he did or didn't admire.

Suddenly he paused in the middle of praising his favorite pitcher.

"You watch baseball with your husband?"

"I'm not married. What I know about baseball I picked up from my father."

"Your father's a fan? Which team?"

"He used to like the Texas Rangers."

"Who does he like now?"

"I think I told you last time that my father died."

"Oh yeah, I forgot. You said a car crash. And your mother was killed too, you said."

She was surprised. Something of their unsatisfactory talk had stayed with him.

"I also told you I had a sister, remember?"

He nodded. "Yeah. You have a shop in Old Town, you said."

"Do you have any brothers or sisters, Herman?"

Suddenly he seemed angry. "I told you last time I got no family."

"I'm sorry, We both forgot some of the things we said last week. Maybe because it wasn't much of a visit."

He cast her a long look before speaking again.

"I might have a sister somewhere, unless she's dead."

Some innate sense told her not to probe. The sense was right. He was already asking her an unrelated question.

"You and your sister, you live together?"

"Yes. She was badly injured in the accident that killed our parents. She's in a wheelchair."

"She can't walk or nothing? Who takes care of her when you're not home?"

Deirdre told him about Yolanda and added, "My sister can't walk, but that doesn't keep her from helping me in the shop. I believe I told you she paints beautiful shirts with Indian designs. We sell them in the shop."

An idea sprang into her mind.

"Would you like me to bring you one of the shirts next time I come?"

An expression of surprise crossed his face.

"You mean, give me a shirt, for myself, to wear?"

"Yes."

His surprised expression had given way to a pleased look.

"Yeah, sure."

"All right. I'll have my sister paint a Sun kachina for you. That's the most popular design—I know you'll like it."

She described the design and watched a flicker of interest appear in his eyes.

A few minutes later the guard announced the end of visiting time.

"I'll see you next week, Herman," Deirdre said.

His reply was little more than a grunt. "Yeah."

But the hostility was gone from his eyes.

Back in the shop, Candy greeted her with a curious look.

"Guess who was in here while you were gone!"

Deirdre felt a quick stirring of her heart. *Gordon?* But Candy's next words turned the stirring into a pang of surprise and anger.

"It was Paul."

From a dark corner of her mind it all came to light—the handsome face, the dark, deep-set eyes, the crisp black hair.... And the memory of his cruel words.

"What did he want?"

"He said he'd been meaning to come in and see the shop ever since he heard we'd opened it, but he's been out of town a lot on business."

She imagined Paul running into someone they both knew, one of the few mutual friends who hadn't faded out of her life with the breakup. She pictured him being told that Candy was much better and was a working partner in the shop. He had to see for himself.

"He was disappointed you weren't here," Candy was saying.

"Did you tell him where I'd gone?"

"Yes." Candy's face grew troubled. "I hope that was okay."

"Sure it's okay; why wouldn't it be?"

"After I told him, I thought maybe you might not want him knowing every little thing you've been up to since you broke up."

"I don't give a hoot what he does or doesn't know," Deirdre said.

Candy looked at her thoughtfully.

"I still don't know why you didn't marry him, Dee Dee."

"Do you wish I had?" Deirdre knew she was evading the implied question, but Candy must never know the reason.

Candy answered with a question of her own. "Do you still have feelings for him?"

"Not like I had when we were engaged," she said.

It was true. Knowing he'd been in the shop that day had dredged up some good memories, but thoughts of his insensitivity had far outnumbered them.

"I only asked because I think he still has a thing for you," Candy said. "He was really disappointed you weren't here and sorry he couldn't wait till you got back."

"Well, maybe he'll drop in again sometime."

Deirdre hung her sweater and purse on a hook

in the back room. As far as she was concerned, the discussion had ended.

Candy was quick to pick up on this.

"How'd it go with the inmate today?"

"Oh, much better. He opened up a lot—especially when I promised to bring him one of your kachina shirts."

"Oh, great!" Candy's smile belied her rueful tone. "Now I'm going to be the convicts' couturier. What size is he?"

"Better make it a large. He's a small kid but he's stocky."

"What did you talk about besides the shirt?"

"Baseball, mostly."

"Didn't he tell you anything about himself—his family?"

"He said he had no family, but then he said something rather strange. He said he might have a sister somewhere unless she'd died. I didn't question him about it. Maybe next time he'll explain."

"Did he tell you why he's in prison?"

"No, but I'm sure he'll open up in time."

Some customers came into the shop just then and asked to see rings. While they were looking over a tray, she thought of Gordon.

Remembering that night, nearly a week ago, she could almost feel the gentle touch of his hand on her face. He'd said he'd see her soon. Why hadn't he come into the shop or telephoned? Had he been thinking about the party, remembering how she'd avoided dancing with him most of the evening? Had he figured out she was making sure there'd be no more chances of their drawing closer in mind and heart? Did he suspect there was something holding her back from falling in love?

She rang up the customers' purchase and handed them the package.

The minute they were gone, Candy looked questioningly at her. "What's on your mind, Dee Dee? You look like you're doing some heavy thinking."

"I can't imagine why you'd say that."

"You're not fooling me—you were thinking about Gordon, weren't you?"

Deirdre had to smile. "All right, I was."

"He'll show up again soon," Candy said, "and when he does, I certainly hope you'll give him more encouragement than you did at the party."

Chapter Four

It was almost closing time, two days later, when Deirdre saw the familiar Western hat looming in the shop doorway. A moment later, Gordon was smiling at her across the counter.

"Hi."

"Hello, stranger," she said, then thought she shouldn't have said that. He might think she'd missed him.

"I've been on a different schedule at the hospital," he said. "By the time I was free I knew you'd be closed. I would have called you at home, but I didn't have your number and you're not in the book."

"We're unlisted. I'm sorry I didn't think to give you our number."

Why had she said that? It would only encourage him, and she had no intentions of following Candy's advice.

"I guess you're going to close up soon," he said. "How about going for something to eat?"

"Oh, I can't," she said. "I've got to go home and get Candy's dinner. Yolanda went home early today."

As Deirdre spoke the picture came to her mind of Candy wheeling around the kitchen, opening the refrigerator, setting the table, stirring pots on the stove. Candy was well able to prepare her own dinner. If she should find out how she was being used, she wouldn't like it. And she'd be sure to find out. Gordon would make some chance remark during one of his visits to the shop.

"Well—if we don't take too long. . . ." she said, and watched the disappointment drain from his eyes.

"Great. Is there something I can do to help you close up?"

She set him to work taking jewelry out of the showcase and putting it in the safe in the back room. She busied herself with the day's receipts. Then she phoned Candy.

"I'm glad you're finally beginning to realize I don't need a constant baby-sitter," Candy said. "Have fun. Say hello to Gordon for me."

Gordon and Deirdre walked across the plaza to a small café that served French food. Deirdre was acquainted with the owner, an elderly gentleman named Claude who boasted he'd once been a chef in a four-star Parisian restaurant. He greeted them warmly and led them to a table in a dimly lit corner.

"This will do?" he asked, silvery mustache quivering above a knowing smile.

"Yes, Claude, this is fine," Deirdre replied.

When he was out of earshot, she looked across the table at Gordon and laughed.

"I know this is the darkest table in the place, but Claude has the romantic French viewpoint of seeing a young man with a young woman and thinking something must be going on."

"They're probably right ninety-nine percent of the time," Gordon said, picking up the menu.

His words caught her off guard. She made no reply, but began to study her own menu.

Claude took their order himself.

"That's quite an honor," Deirdre explained to Gordon. "It means he considers us special patrons of his establishment."

"How long have you known him?"

"Since Candy and I were kids. Our parents used to bring us here often. He's always taken an interest in us."

"I hope he approves of me," Gordon said.

She pretended she hadn't heard this. Instead, she turned her attention to eating.

"Mine's very good. How is yours?" she asked.

"Tasty. I've always liked French cooking."

"So have I."

This was a safe subject, she thought. It could be drawn out—perhaps extended till the end of the meal.

"There aren't many French restaurants out here," she said. "I guess New York has a lot of them."

"Yes, they're all over Manhattan. My favorite was a tiny place in a basement on a side street in midtown. Wonderful onion soup. Always made me think of a big kitchen in a Normandy farmhouse with a big pot simmering on the back of a stove and a French housewife taking long, crusty loaves of bread out of the oven."

"Why Gordon—that's almost poetic!" she teased. "Have you ever been in France?"

"Not yet. It's on my list of places I want to see someday. Mexico's on the list too, and now that I'm out here I intend to make a trip down there soon. I suppose you've been there, living so close."

"Yes. Our parents took us several times. The last time we went down the baja to Cabo San Lucas."

"You were a very close family, weren't you?"

"We were. Our mother and father were more than two people who raised us—they were our friends."

He gave her a searching look.

"You and Candy have both adjusted remarkably well to losing them."

"If we have, it's because our father taught us the futility of dwelling on something that can't be changed."

"I wish I'd known your father. I think I'd have liked him."

Her reply sprang from her heart before she could weigh the words.

"He'd have liked you too, Gordon."

He reached across the table and took her hand in his.

"Would he have liked me better than you do, Deirdre?"

How quickly their conversation had strayed from safe topics! It was as though any talk between them would always lead them to this point. She managed a cool reply.

"Gordon, you know I wouldn't be here with you if I didn't like you a lot."

"Sure—but you tried to get out of it by saying you had to go home to take care of Candy."

She attempted to draw her hand away, but he held it firmly.

"Deirdre, we both know there's something

happening with us and we both know you're fighting it. Why?"

I should tell him about Paul, she thought. But telling him would be saying she was now turned off by all men—incapable of relating to anyone else. How archaic that would sound—like the heroine in some nineteenth-century novel.

Yet, she sensed something of an ultimatum in the way he held her hand and asked "why?"

"Can't we just be good friends?" she asked.

The look in his eyes was as inescapable as the grasp of his hand.

"Sure, Deirdre, if that's what you want."

She nodded, unable to trust her voice, and tried to justify her affirmation in her own mind.

To give up her heart again would be to risk its second shattering. She was in control of her life now. The anguish of bereavement and the sorrow of Candy's disability were lessening, and her disillusionment with Paul lingered only as a reminder of what could happen again.

She didn't know how long she'd been silent. But now the cold emptiness of her hand made her realize Gordon had released it.

At that moment Claude appeared to remove their plates and ask if they wanted dessert or coffee.

Gordon glanced at his watch.

"I guess you want to get going, Deirdre."

"Yes." She smiled at Claude. "Another time we'll stay for coffee and enjoy your wonderful pastries."

This was as much for Gordon's benefit as it was for Claude's. She knew she hadn't given Gordon a straight answer. She wanted him to know she wasn't shutting him out of her life.

"Can't we be friends?" It was the classic brush-off. But now she couldn't bear the thought of never seeing him again.

They walked in silence to her car.

"Please come around to the shop soon," she said. "We didn't have much time to talk tonight. I want to tell you about my latest visit with the prison inmate."

"Sure, I'll be around," he replied.

On her drive home his parting words sounded over and over in her mind. They were innocuous words, depending on the tone of voice for their true meaning.

"Sure, I'll be around." Spoken with sarcasm, this could have meant he'd be around when Niagara Falls ran dry. But his voice had conveyed a clear and simple message.

He had no intention of dropping out of her life.

Herman was already in the visitors' area when Deirdre arrived for their next talk. She thought she saw a trace of worry on his face.

"Am I late?" she asked.

"Nope. They just now let me in here."

He eyed the paper sack she was carrying.

"Is that the shirt?"

"Yes. It made a big hit with the guard who examined it. I hope you like it too."

She took the shirt out of the bag and held it up.

"How's this, Herman?"

"It looks good," he replied. For the first time, she saw a full smile come to his face.

She passed the shirt to him. He immediately put it on over his T-shirt, and she couldn't help thinking how times had changed. In old movies on television, when James Cagney and George Raft were imprisoned, they had to wear black-and-white striped uniforms. Now, if he wanted to, a convicted felon could wear a blue denim shirt with a Hopi kachina painted on it.

"Does it fit?" she asked. "If not, I can have my sister do another in the right size."

"It fits good," he said.

Deirdre knew they couldn't go on talking about the shirt for the entire visit.

"I've been thinking of you during the baseball games. I guess you've been watching on television."

"Yeah, it's going good so far."

"I don't really know much about the play-offs," she said. "Maybe you could explain what's going on."

He spent a few minutes enlightening her about teams and their current standings in the leagues. He spoke admiringly of the skill of one of his favorite players.

"When he has the ball in his hand he knows right away what to do with it," Herman said.

Then, as though he'd surprised himself by talking so much, he broke into a feeble grin.

"Looks like I done all the talking this time. Now it's your turn."

"What would you like to hear about?"

"Like, where you live and what kind of house you have."

She told him about the foothills, describing the way the house nestled into the mountainside.

"My father was an architect. He designed the house himself, especially for the land. It's a very unusual house with a big glass observatory on top. In winter, when the trees are bare, the observatory can be seen for miles around."

"You got a lot of woods out there, right?"

"Oh, yes. Our own land is about twenty acres. Most of it we left natural, but we do have gardens and a swimming pool. Our father designed the pool too. It's surrounded by rocks and boulders so it looks like a real pond. Next time I come, I'll bring some photos to show you."

"I guess your old man had plenty of dough."

"Whatever he had, he worked hard for, most of his life."

"But you and your sister—you got his money now, right?"

He was getting a bit too inquisitive, she thought. Aloud, she said, "We have enough to be comfortable."

"I guess you and your sister got your education," he said. "Me, I dropped out of school. I wish I hadn't. I wish I'd gone back and finished, but there wasn't nobody to tell me to."

"Isn't there a program here so you could get your high school equivalency certificate?"

"Yeah, they told me about that."

"Then you should get with it, Herman."

He shrugged. "Why?"

"Because, if you really wanted to, by the time you're released you could have the equivalency of a high school diploma. Then you'd have a good chance of making something of yourself and having a better life. Others have done it—why not you?"

He was staring at her with an expression she couldn't define.

"What's the matter, Herman?"

"I was just thinking you talk like my sister."

"That's the sister you mentioned—you said she might be out there somewhere...."

"Yeah—Rita. But she's probably dead." He looked away for a moment. "She was the only one who ever cared about me."

Deirdre knew she must not push. She waited for him to go on.

A moment later he was telling her about a childhood of deprivation, a household bare of basic comforts, further impoverished by irresponsible, abusive parents, and about two children who'd clung together for solace.

"Rita and me, we was little kids when our old man left us and never came back. We was on welfare and our ma was boozed up most of the time. When she died, I remember the old woman upstairs saying she drank herself to death. Rita and me, we was put in separate foster homes. That was six years ago. I never seen my sister again."

Deirdre was at a loss for words. What sort of comment could be made on such a heartrending story? She imagined what had happened to Herman during the past six years—an unruly, incorrigible adolescent deteriorating into a street punk, then becoming a full-fledged criminal.

She could only guess why a brother and sister would be separated, never to see each other

again. There might have been difficulty finding
one suitable foster home for two adolescents.
Perhaps the homes were too far apart for visits
or perhaps communication was not encouraged.
Rita might have been legally adopted and taken
out of state. Whatever the reason, Deirdre was
certain Herman's present predicament was the
result.

His voice broke into her contemplation.

"I didn't mean to lay all this on you."

He wasn't apologizing. It was as if he were
angry at himself for opening up to her. Suddenly
some of his old hostility seemed to have returned.

"You want to know how long I'm in for?"

"I didn't ask you, Herman, but if you want to
tell me ..."

"Five years. You want to know what for? Me
and two guys ripped off a liquor store and the
owner was shot."

He waited, his eyes searching her face. When
she made no reply, he spoke again.

"I know what you're thinking—was he shot
dead and did I do it? Well, it's 'no' to both."

"I'm relieved to hear that, Herman. How did
you get involved with the other two?"

"In the pool hall after I dropped out of school.
We had been hanging out for a while before we
was busted. We still hang out together in here."

"They're here, in this prison?"

"Yeah."

Deirdre saw the guard approaching.

"It looks like our time is up," she said. "I'll see you next week, Herman."

"Yeah," he replied. "Don't forget to bring the pictures of your house."

Because Candy had stayed home to keep an appointment with her physical therapist, the shop had been closed during Deirdre's visit with Herman.

On her way along the walk, she called a greeting through the open door of Ralph's shop and paused until he appeared.

"Nobody around while you were gone—not even lookers," he told her. "But things will pick up in a day or two, for sure."

She knew he was referring to the annual hot-air balloon festival held in Albuquerque the first week of October, an event that was always a big tourist attraction.

The spectacle of several hundred colorful balloons in mass ascension at daybreak was something Gordon would enjoy, she thought. She wondered if he were planning to go.

While she was opening the shop, memories arose of being taken to the launch site on the first morning of the festival, she and Candy, two excited little girls bundled up in warm sweaters and caps against the predawn chill. Their mother had brought along a thermos of cocoa for them and coffee for herself and their father. The girls had taken turns riding on his shoulders.

The wonder of the spectacle had faded with her childhood. It was enough, in later years, to view the balloons scattered in the sky throughout the week of the festival.

Now she found herself wanting to renew the excitement of the launch. With reluctance, she admitted she wanted to share it with Gordon.

It had been nearly a week since she'd told him she wanted only his friendship. Had she imagined the promise in his reply?

"I'll be around..."

Perhaps his schedule rotation had made it impossible for him to come to the shop. But no matter what his duty hours were, he could have reached her by phone, here or at home.

Then she remembered he still didn't have her home number.

The sound of the phone pierced her thoughts. The voice on the line turned her heart to stone.

"Is that you, Dee?"

She took a deep breath. "Hello, Paul."

"I tried to call you earlier but there was no answer. So I called you at home and Candy said you were doing that prison volunteer thing and to try later, so here I am. I guess Candy told you I was in the shop last week."

"Yes, she did."

"I was surprised to see her looking so well—a big improvement since I saw her last."

Deep inside her, Deirdre felt a swell of anger.

"Is there something I can do for you, Paul?"

"You're wondering why I called you, aren't you? I want to see you, Dee. I've missed you."

She choked back the words she wanted to say—that she didn't want to see him and she hadn't missed him—lest her anger come through too clearly.

"I don't think there's much point in our seeing each other," she managed to say.

"Don't be like that, Dee. You know we had a good thing going, and now there's no reason why we can't have it again."

"I don't think so, Paul."

"Look—I'd much rather discuss this in person than over the phone. I'm going out of town on business for a few days, but I'll be in touch when I get back."

After she'd hung up the phone, she sat staring at it, her mind in a whirl of confusion. Why, after all this time, did Paul expect he could come back into her life? What had he meant when he'd said *now* there was no reason why they couldn't have what they'd had before?

She should have made it clear to him that she didn't want to see him. But even if she had, Paul was a handsome man and he knew it. In his arrogance, he probably thought that if they met face-to-face, she'd be drawn to him again—captivated by his charm and fabulous good looks. He had no idea how his basic insensitivity had shadowed his outward appearance.

She realized her disillusionment had grown greater with the sound of his voice, and she felt the rising of something akin to hatred. If Paul hadn't reentered her life this way, in time she might have opened her heart to Gordon. Now all her bitterness, all her distrust, had been reinforced.

When she saw Gordon again she knew she must tell him, once and for all, that she wanted nothing more than his friendship.

Chapter Five

The following afternoon Gordon came into the shop.

Seeing him again sent Deirdre's heart racing. She tried to calm herself before greeting him.

"It's good to see you, Gordon. How are things going?"

"Okay. Busy, as usual."

"I hope you're not too busy to stay and visit a while."

He smiled ruefully. "Sorry—I can only stay a few minutes. I wanted to ask you to go to the balloon festival with me tomorrow morning for the mass ascension."

Taken by surprise, she could think of no excuse not to agree. The liftoff would take place at daybreak—plenty of time for her to get to the shop afterwards. Yolanda would be with Candy. And being outdoors in the cold in a big crowd could not by any stretch of the imagination be considered romantic. They'd be just two good friends enjoying the event together.

"I'd like to go, Gordon. I haven't been out there to see the ascension in years."

"I'll pick you up at quarter to five tomorrow morning," he said. "Jake and Amy are meeting us at the site, and they've invited us back to their place for breakfast afterward."

How good that sounded!

"I wish I could hang around a while, but I've got to get back to the hospital," he said, turning towards the door.

"Why didn't you give me a call instead of coming over here?"

He looked at her with a playful grin.

"I thought the chances of you saying 'yes' would be better if I asked you in person."

She couldn't help laughing.

"Maybe you were right. Thanks for asking me, Gordon."

After he'd gone, she felt a surge of anticipation. But it was nostalgia, she told herself—a throwback to the times when she'd gone out to view the balloons with Candy and their parents. It really didn't have anything to do with Gordon.

* * *

At five-thirty the following morning, the launch site was busy with balloon crews readying their crafts and with crowds of spectators watching the firing.

"I guess this is old stuff to you," Gordon said.

"It doesn't seem like old stuff," Deirdre replied. "It's just as exciting now as it ever was."

She tried to thrust aside the feeling that much of the excitement came from driving down from the foothills with Gordon in the darkness, knowing that for a few hours they'd be together.

"Keep an eye out for Jake and Amy," Gordon was saying. "They should be around here somewhere."

A moment later they saw them—Jake with his elder son riding on his shoulders, Amy with the younger boy sound asleep in a stroller.

Seeing them gave Deirdre a strange longing. They looked so complete.

"This is so exciting," Amy said. "We've never seen anything like this before. But I suppose you've been here many times, haven't you, Deirdre?"

"She told me she's just as excited about it now as she was when she was a kid," Gordon said. "I'm thankful for that. I'm having enough trouble getting her to go out with me without taking her on a boring date."

As he spoke, he linked arms with Deirdre and smiled down at her. It was a warm, playful gesture, and she felt herself responding by smiling back at him.

"She wouldn't smile at you that way if she'd been giving you any trouble," Jake said, laughing.

Then Deirdre heard Gordon's voice—low, almost a whisper. "Didn't I tell you, you have a million-dollar smile!"

Jake was taking a thermos of coffee and some paper cups out of a knapsack.

"We brought this along. It will hold us till breakfast."

"Daddy, may I have some of that?" asked the little boy on his shoulders.

"You may have some juice, buddy," Jake replied. He pulled out a small plastic container, opened it, and handed it up to the boy. Then he looked at Amy.

"Does the little guy show any signs of waking up?"

"He's still out like a light. Better have his juice ready, though. He might come to any minute and we both know what that means!"

Deirdre heard the love in Amy's voice and saw it in the look she and Jake exchanged. Again she was struck with the thought that, despite their lack of material possessions, Amy and Jake had it all.

Now tentative streaks of daylight shone in the sky, and the first few balloons were filled and struggling from their prone positions. More followed until the field was covered with rising patches of color, and then it was sunup and all at once they were off, crowding the sky with a mass of shapes and hues.

"I wouldn't have missed this for anything," Gordon said to Deirdre. "I'd have come anyway, but seeing this with you makes it special."

She longed to tell him he'd spoken her own thoughts. If only Paul had not reappeared to remind her of the disillusionment and bitterness of a trust betrayed....

Amy and Jake's kitchen was flooded with sunshine by the time they arrived at the little house on Amherst Street.

The younger child was at the table in his high chair, banging a spoon and gnawing on a piece of toast. His older brother had fallen asleep in the car and Jake had put him to bed.

"That's the way it goes," Amy said. "It would be nice if we could put both of them down for a nap at the same time and have a peaceful, adult breakfast, but when one's asleep the other's awake. They never seem to synchronize."

"At least nobody's whining or crying at the moment," Jake said. He was at the stove, stirring one skillet and watching another.

"What's cooking, Doc?" Gordon asked.

"It's fake bacon and eggs," Jake replied. "Amy insists on it." He cast a grin at Amy, who was setting the table. "It's really not bad, though. Tastes almost like the real thing."

"And much better for your health," Amy added. "Both of our fathers died of heart disease and we both remember how they used to have bacon or sausage with eggs for breakfast every day. I want Jake around to see our kids grown up."

"I'd like to have someone looking after me that way," Gordon said.

He glanced at Deirdre as he spoke. She avoided his eyes.

"It looks like you're ready to dish up, Jake," she said. "Let me help."

She held the plates while he filled them, then put them on the table.

After they'd eaten, Deirdre helped Amy clean up the kitchen while the men went into the living room with the child.

"Deirdre, we're glad you and Gordon found each other," Amy said.

Deirdre stared at her, not sure how to reply.

"Am I assuming something I shouldn't?" Amy

asked. "Jake and I thought we saw all the signs. If we're mistaken, I apologize."

"There's no need for an apology, Amy. Gordon and I have become very good friends and I'm glad, too, that we found each other."

Amy immediately turned to another subject.

"Gordon told us you'd been doing volunteer visiting at the prison. How's it going?"

"It was discouraging at first, but now it's getting better."

She gave Amy an account of her progress with Herman.

"He doesn't sound to me like he's a hardened criminal," Amy commented.

"I don't believe he is. I think it might have been a case of a kid falling in with the wrong company. I hope I can help him realize that."

Amy smiled. "Gordon's right about you. You're a good person, Deirdre."

"No more than average," Deirdre replied. She felt a bit embarrassed. It sounded as though Gordon had done some talking about her to Jake and Amy.

Amy put the last dish away in the cabinet and turned to Deirdre with another smile.

"I'd say your devotion to your sister is well above average."

For a moment, Deirdre thought Amy somehow

knew about the situation with Paul, but her next words dispelled the idea.

"Gordon told us how difficult it's been for him to spend some time with you—how you always feel you must get home to Candy. Not many women would cut a date short with a man like Gordon, for any kind of reason."

She cast an uncertain look at Deirdre and added, "There's more than one student nurse at the hospital who'd love to date Gordon."

Deirdre felt her heart sink.

"Why not?" she said. "He's a very attractive man."

She hoped the tone of her voice sounded lighter than her heart felt at that moment.

"Well, let's go and join the men," Amy said.

In the living room, Deirdre glanced at her watch.

"I should be going home to get my car. I have to open the shop in an hour or so."

"There's no need for you to go home for your car," Gordon said. "I'll take you to the shop from here."

"But I'll need my car to get home after I close up."

Gordon turned to Jake with a wry smile.

"See what I mean by trouble? I thought this would be a sneaky way of seeing her later, but she's too fast for me."

They all laughed and Deirdre decided there would be no harm in having him pick her up at the shop and take her home. She'd tell him, on the way out to the foothills, that she wanted nothing more than his friendship.

He drove her to Old Town and told her he'd be back at six.

She phoned Candy as soon as she entered the shop.

"You're probably wondering why I didn't come back for my car," she said. "I—"

Candy didn't wait to hear the explanation.

"I wasn't wondering at all," she said. "I figured Gordon would drop you off at the shop and bring you home later. Did you have a good time?"

"It was really great."

Two customers entered the shop.

"I have to ring off now, Candy. I'll see you tonight."

"Wait a second," Candy said. "Ask Gordon to stay for dinner when he drives you home. I'll wheedle Yolanda into making something special."

Before Deirdre could reply, Candy had said good-bye.

Deirdre told herself she'd call Candy back as soon as she was finished with the customers and tell her she wasn't inviting Gordon for dinner. But it developed into such a busy day that she

barely had time to heat up a can of soup in the
back room for lunch. Before she had a minute
to pick up the phone, it was late afternoon.

Yolanda would have already put together that
something special. And because Candy had told
her there'd be a man at the table, she'd have
made enough to feed an army.

There was nothing to do but accept the fact
that Gordon was going to have dinner in her
home tonight.

A sudden thought flashed in her mind. Suppose he already had plans for dinner? Suppose
he had a date with one of those student nurses
Amy had mentioned? She could almost see the
pretty face and the curly blond, or maybe glossy
black, hair beneath a starched cap, and a gorgeous figure filling out a uniform in all the right
places.

When he came for her at closing time, she was
almost afraid to extend Candy's invitation, but
when she did he looked at her in pleased surprise
and said he'd be delighted.

"What brought this on?" he asked when they
were on their way.

"Actually, it was Candy's suggestion," she began to say, then, not wishing to hurt his feelings,
added, "I should have thought of it myself. I'm
glad you were free this evening."

"I'll always be free for you," he said.

She hastily called his attention to the colorful foliage on either side of the highway.

"I think the autumn color's at its peak, don't you? The view from our observatory is beautiful. It's like looking down on acres and acres of gold. I'll show you when we get there."

The minute the words were out of her mouth she regretted them. Being in the observatory with Gordon, sharing the wondrous sight of the golden mountainside, watching the sun leaving its fiery trail over the western slopes, was something she shouldn't risk.

Candy greeted them at the door, all smiles.

"Yolanda made a scrumptious Indian dish. Before she left, she said to let it cook a few more minutes. Why don't you show Gordon the view from the observatory while there's still daylight, Dee Dee?"

They climbed the circular stair to the top of the house. Just as she knew it would be, the sight was breathtaking. And just as she'd feared, or perhaps hoped, he took her hand in his and they savored the magic of the autumn twilight together.

"Isn't it beautiful?" she asked.

"You're beautiful," he said.

She trembled, knowing in her heart what could follow. She tried to head it off.

"Oh Gordon, we both know I'm not really beautiful."

"You are to me," he whispered, and then his arms were around her and she felt his kiss, gentle and tender, and all her past determination couldn't keep her from responding.

When the kiss ended, he held her close in his arms and she could almost hear his next words. She sensed them rushing toward her like an incoming tide and she could do nothing to stop them. A moment later they'd flooded her heart.

"I love you, Deirdre."

He didn't wait for her to answer, but placed his hand beneath her chin, lifting her face, looking into her eyes.

"I just wanted to establish that fact," he said. "Now, let's go down—Candy's waiting."

It was clear he didn't expect any kind of reply. It was as if he'd sensed her heart was in conflict and he'd sought to bring some order into it.

Somehow she got through the meal. The light banter and the laughter couldn't block out the memory of Gordon telling her he loved her, yet he gave no sign that their tender moments in the observatory had happened at all.

When the time came for him to leave, he gave both women a warm hug and Deirdre could see no expression on his face to remind her of what he'd told her. It was as he'd said—he wanted to establish the fact. No pressure, no expectations, just a plain, simple truth for her to deal with as she would.

Inexplicably, she found herself thinking how Herman might describe the situation.

Like the baseball player he admired, she had the ball in her hand. But she didn't know what to do with it, and this wasn't a game—this was her life, and it was her own heart she was holding.

Chapter Six

The first words out of Herman's mouth when Deirdre paid her next visit were, "Did you bring the pictures?"

How sad, she thought, that he had no one else to bring him photographs—pictures of his own house, his own family.

"Yes, I have them here," she replied. She handed the first one to him.

"This is a shot of the house taken from down in the valley. The trees hide most of it, but you can see the observatory plainly."

"I never seen a house like that," he said.

"That's because it's one of a kind. There's not another like it in Albuquerque or anywhere else."

She passed him another photo of the front of the house, taken from across the driveway. He immediately commented on Yolanda's old, solid-sided van parked near the garage.

"Is that your van?"

"No, it belongs to the woman I told you about who comes in to help."

"Have you got a shot of the pool?"

"Sure." She handed him two pictures of Candy swimming.

"I thought you said your sister was in a wheel-chair."

"She is, most of the time. But swimming is part of her physical therapy."

She handed him two more pictures.

"Here's our living room. That's our dog Perro lying in front of the fireplace."

"I like the fireplace."

"It *is* beautiful, isn't it? It's built of native rocks."

"You told me your dog is part coyote. Is he mean?"

"Not really. He barks and snarls at anyone he hears at the door, but if someone calls him by name he turns into a pussycat."

"I like dogs."

"They're great pets and wonderful compan-ions. We've had Perro since he was a puppy."

She handed him the remaining picture—a

shot of Yolanda standing in the kitchen with Candy nearby in her wheelchair.

"Your sister's face got smashed up, didn't it? Did she used to be pretty?"

"Yes, very pretty."

"That woman with her looks Indian. Is she the one who owns that van?"

"Yes, and you're right, she's half Native American. Her father's a Santo Domingo and her mother's Mexican-American."

She put the photos back in her purse.

"That's all you got?" he asked.

"Yes. I didn't think I should bring too many. Looking at pictures can get boring."

"I liked looking at them," he said. "I never seen a house like that, or a pool."

Again she thought it sad that he had to take pleasure in looking at pictures of strangers and places with which he had no connection. How unfortunate he had no one to visit him and bring photographs of home and loved ones.

"I'm glad you enjoyed them, Herman. Next time I come I'll bring some more."

"Can I see that one of your coyote dog again? What did you say his name is—Pedro?"

"Close. It's Perro—you know, 'dog' in Spanish." She opened her purse. "Look at all of them again if you want to."

She handed the photos back to him and watched him linger over them as though he were reluctant to part with them.

A sudden idea entered her mind.

"Herman, would you like to keep the photos till next week?"

He looked pleased. "Yeah."

"You can give them back to me when I see you again," she said.

Candy had a number of shirt orders to fill and hadn't come into the shop that day.

"There'll probably be a lull now that the balloon festival is over," she'd said, "but if you get busy, give me a call and Yolanda can bring me down."

Ralph in the neighboring shop reported that it had been a very slow morning. A good time to do some cleaning and rearranging, Deirdre thought.

She'd finished mopping the brick floor and was spraying glass cleaner on the showcase when she heard the door open. Looking around, she saw Paul. She caught her breath, half startled, half annoyed.

He was regarding her with an amused smile. "You seem surprised, Dee. Didn't I promise you I'd drop in when I had the time?"

She wanted to tell him she'd almost forgotten

his phone call. It was the truth. Her mind had been crowded with thoughts of Gordon. She hadn't seen or heard from him since the night he'd told her exactly how he felt about her. Even now, with Paul standing right there, she couldn't stop thinking about being in Gordon's arms and hearing him say he loved her.

"Hello, Paul," she said. "I'll be with you in a few minutes."

She went into the back room to put away the cleaning supplies and wash her hands.

"You don't have to put on makeup or comb your hair," he called. "You look fine."

He thought she was fixing herself up for him! What arrogance.

"Why didn't you let me know you'd be in today?" she said as she came out of the back room and stood behind the counter. "I would have had my hair done and had a facial."

He appeared not to recognize the sarcasm.

"I'll get right to the point, Dee," he said. "Like I told you on the phone, there's no reason why we can't get back together now. I know you were steamed when I said we should put Candy in a nursing home. I've thought about that a lot since we broke up and I realize I shouldn't have said it, even though you have to admit I was right. It would have been a real drag having to take care of her. And if we had to go somewhere with her, people would stare and whisper."

He leaned over the counter.

"I heard she's having a series of plastic surgeries on her face and that her looks will be almost normal. I also heard she's having an operation next month and she'll soon be walking again."

Deirdre didn't tell him he'd been misinformed—that the operation scheduled for November was not to restore the use of Candy's legs but further surgery on her face.

"Who told you that, Paul?"

"Oh, I heard it at a party. You know how word gets around in this town."

Her anger rose at the thought of Candy's condition being the subject of gossip at a party attended by people who'd dropped out of her life after her breakup with Paul. Her true friends knew what was really happening with Candy.

"So the reason you're here is because you believe Candy wouldn't be a drag anymore—is that it?"

He hesitated. "Well, she'll be walking and she'll have her looks back. . . ."

"How about her seizures, Paul, wouldn't that be a drag?"

She knew she was baiting him. She wanted

to catch him on his own thoughts and have him spew out every hateful one.

"The seizures—I'd almost forgotten," he said. "But they can be controlled by medication, can't they—I mean, she doesn't suddenly...."

"Throw fits? Is that what you were going to say, Paul?"

He stared at her. "Come on, Dee, lighten up. I told you I've missed you and I told you I'm sorry I said what I did. Circumstances have changed and now we can take up where we left off."

Her throat was so choked with anger, she couldn't speak.

"Think back on all the good times we had, Dee," he was saying. "I know you've missed them as much as I have."

"No, Paul, I haven't missed them at all," she managed to say. "And I haven't missed you, either."

"That's your pride talking, Dee—because I took so long to come back into your life."

Suddenly he walked around behind the counter and placed his hands on her shoulders, drawing her close to him. She shoved him away.

"Please don't, Paul. I have no interest in our getting back together. I want you to leave."

He looked at her sharply. "You don't mean that, Dee."

"Yes, I do. I'm seeing someone else."

He threw back his head and laughed. "Oh, Dee—I know and everyone else knows there hasn't been a man in your life since we broke up!"

Neither of them had heard the door to the shop open. Now came the sound of a voice, loud and clear, speaking a single word.

"Wrong!"

Gordon strode towards them, leveling his gaze directly at Paul.

Deirdre saw Paul's eyes take in Gordon's height and build and flicker over the broad-brimmed, Western hat. The only word she could think of to describe the expression on his handsome, arrogant face was Grandmother's favorite—flabbergasted.

She heard herself making introductions. "Gordon Burns, meet Paul Martin." She felt the ripple of a laugh deep within her. How approving Grandmother would be that she could maintain proper social demeanor even in a confrontation! Then, inexplicably, the ripple changed from laughter to tears and she began to tremble, trying to keep them from rising to her eyes.

"I heard the lady tell you she wanted you to leave," Gordon said to Paul.

Paul was already out from behind the counter.

Deirdre heard both anger and arrogance in his reply.

"So it's John Wayne to the rescue, Dee? All right, I'm on my way, but don't bother to call me when you've come to your senses."

Gordon didn't wait for the door to close. He was behind the counter, taking Deirdre into his arms, holding her until she stopped trembling.

"You've been hurt by that man, haven't you, Deirdre?"

She nodded, unable to speak, and he released her from his arms to place his hands on either side of her face and lift it up to meet his eyes.

"I'm not going to ask you what he did. That's for you to tell me in your own time."

For an instant she came close to telling him everything, but the moment passed and he was taking her by the hand, leading her out from behind the counter to a nearby bench.

"I've missed you," he said.

Echoes of Paul's words, she thought, but what Paul had really missed were the trimmings surrounding her. Gordon had missed *her*.

"Can you stay a while?" she asked. She knew he'd understand this was her way of telling him she missed him too.

"I wish I could, but I've got to get back to the hospital. Before I go, though, I want you to give me your home phone number." He took a small notebook out of his pocket.

She gave him the number and said, "I hope having my home number won't keep you from coming into the shop."

"I'll come every chance I get," he replied. He wrote something on a page of the notebook, tore it out, and handed it to her. "Here's the phone number at my apartment, and the other one is the hospital."

Without his saying it, she knew what he meant. He wanted her to call him if she needed him.

"I don't think Paul will bother me again," she said.

"It's not just that. I want you to know where you can reach me, anytime, for any reason."

Then she understood fully. It was another way of letting her know he loved her. He hadn't told her again in so many words, and he wouldn't—not until she, too, opened up her heart.

"You look tired, Dee Dee," Candy said when Deirdre got home that evening. "Was it a busy day after all?"

"It depends on what you'd call 'busy.' This morning there were some Indians around selling jewelry, and my friend Nancy dropped in just to say hello. After I got back from visiting Herman, things were so quiet I decided to clean the shop and while I was doing that, Paul came in and—"

"Paul was there? What happened?"

"He wanted to get back together but I told him I wasn't interested. He got very insistent and wasn't about to take no for an answer when Gordon appeared."

She described the confrontation.

"Well, I'd say you had quite a day," Candy said. "Sit down and relax. While I'm putting dinner on the table you can tell me what's going on with you and Gordon."

"There's really nothing going on," Deirdre replied.

Candy cast her a doubting smile.

"Let me get this straight. Paul tells you he wants to come back and gives you a hard time when you tell him to get lost, and Gordon arrives just in time to kick him out. That sure as shooting sounds to me like there's something going on."

Deirdre knew she couldn't hide her conflict from Candy much longer. Short of revealing the reason for her breakup with Paul, she had to confide some of her feelings and stretch the truth a little.

"I found out Paul wasn't really in love with me," she said. "I was terribly hurt and now I'm finding it hard to develop serious feelings for anyone else."

"He must have loved you, or he wouldn't have wanted to marry you," Candy said.

Deirdre gave a wry smile. "Because he's an architect, I think he was attracted to what Daddy might be able to do for his career. That, and all the other material things surrounding me, made me look good to him."

"When did you decide that?"

"I guess it came on gradually. Anyway, I'm thankful I realized before the wedding that he didn't really love me."

"This doesn't make sense to me," Candy said. "If he didn't love you, why does he want to come back now?"

Deirdre had no ready answer. She couldn't risk revealing to Candy why she'd broken her engagement to Paul.

"I'm too tired tonight to come up with a reason," she said. "Maybe tomorrow I'll be able to think more clearly."

"I hope in the morning your head will be clear where Gordon is concerned," Candy said.

Later, while Deirdre was helping her get to bed, Candy expressed further thoughts on the subject.

"Dee Dee, if you don't want Paul back in your

life, why are you holding yourself away from Gordon?"

"I told you, I'm wary. Anyway, you're reading too much into my relationship with Gordon. We're just good friends."

"That's baloney and you know it," Candy said. "There's something you're not telling me."

Deirdre felt a tremor of apprehension. Candy was getting entirely too close to suspecting the truth.

Before she could think of a reply, she heard the telephone ringing in her own bedroom across the hall.

"That might be Mr. Gillespie wanting to find out how I'm doing at the prison," she said. She smoothed the bedding around Candy. "Sleep well."

"You too," Candy replied. "Sweet dreams. I hope they're all about Gordon!"

Deirdre answered the phone to Gordon's voice. The sound of it first quickened her heart, then warmed it.

"See what happens when you give your number to strange men?" he said.

"I was hoping you'd call soon, Gordon."

It was true. Ever since he'd taken her number, that thought had been lurking in a corner of her mind.

"I'm on a new schedule and I won't get to the

shop all this week," he said. "But I have a day off coming up after that, and I was wondering if Candy could handle the shop while we drove up to Santa Fe for the day."

The thought of walking across the old plaza with him, window-shopping in the quaint shops along the brick walkways, showing him churches built centuries ago, was too much to resist. She told him she'd like to go.

"I'll ask Yolanda to help Candy in the shop," she said.

From the sound of his voice she could picture the happiness in his eyes.

"That's great. I'll let you know what day as soon as the new rotation comes out. I have to go now. Good night...."

She heard the unspoken words as clearly as if he'd said them.

"I love you, Deirdre."

She lay awake for a long time that night.

Gordon had spoken his mind and heart, but she knew if she were ever to hear those words again—if she were ever to be in his arms again— she must be the one to make the next move.

But first she must rid herself of the doubts which were keeping them apart.

Before sleep came, she prayed for everything to work out.

* * *

The week passed quickly, perhaps because Gordon had called her every night. Some calls were hasty, made during time snatched out of a busy night. Others were longer.

He told her about the Indian child he'd been attending in the hospital—a little girl, four years old, suffering from severe anemia. The compassion in his voice was so intense, Deirdre could almost feel it.

She told him about her last visit with Herman and how she'd left the pictures with him.

"I had no idea he'd enjoy looking at them so much," she said. "He was so pleased when I said he could keep them till next week."

Now the week had passed and it was time for another visit to the prison. She entered the visitors' room with her spirits high. She was certain she had helped Herman.

He came in just as she arrived. Something about the way he greeted her disturbed her. He didn't look at her directly, but averted his eyes, just as he had the first time she'd visited.

"Is everything okay, Herman?"

"Yeah, sure." He shifted in his chair.

"I guess you were pleased that your team made the World Series."

"Yeah."

"Do you think they'll win it?"

He shrugged. "I guess they got a good shot."

She couldn't seem to draw him into any sort of conversation. Strange—he'd been almost talkative last week when she'd shown him the pictures. Then she remembered she hadn't brought along more, as she'd told him she would.

"Herman, I'm sorry, but I forgot to bring you more photos."

He cast her a glance she could not define.

"How's your sister?" he asked suddenly.

"She's doing very well."

"She in your shop today?"

"No, she's been staying home lately, working on her shirts. I closed up the shop while I came over here. Business has slowed down a little, but it always picks up again in the weeks before Christmas."

"She's staying home tomorrow too?"

"Yes. She has a lot of orders to fill. Her shirts keep the shop going when things get slow."

"But she's not there alone. That Indian woman with the van comes every day."

"That's right." She couldn't help smiling. He had the typical young man's interest in cars. Even when she'd shown him the picture of the front of the house, he'd noticed Yolanda's van.

Then she remembered he hadn't given her back the photos.

"Herman, before it slips my mind—may I have my pictures?"

He seemed uneasy. Again, he averted his eyes.

"I forgot to put them in my pocket when they brought me in."

This was why he was behaving so strangely, she decided. He thought she'd be annoyed with him.

"That's all right, Herman," she said. "We both forgot the pictures today, didn't we? You can return them to me next time."

Now, suddenly, he was staring at her.

"You talk nice to me, like my sister."

"I remember you told me that. I hope I can be like a sister to you, Herman."

He turned his head, brushing his hand across his eyes.

"I don't feel so good today."

"Do you feel sick?"

"Yeah—like I was coming down with something."

"Maybe you'd better go back to your room and have someone tell the doctor."

"Back to my *cell,* you mean," he said. "Yeah, that's what I should do."

He rose from his chair. "Thanks for coming. Thanks for everything, uh, Deirdre."

It was the first time he'd spoken her name. She hadn't been sure if he even remembered it.

"I'll see you next time," she said. "I hope you feel better."

"Yeah," he replied, and turned to go.

Chapter Seven

The days were getting shorter, Deirdre thought as she drove home from the shop the following day. Only last week it was still light when she reached the foothills. Now it was almost dark.

Turning into the driveway, she noticed that Yolanda's van wasn't parked in its usual place. Odd, she thought, because Yolanda had said that her husband had gone on an overnight hunting trip and she was going to spend the night here.

Deirdre put her car away and entered the house through the door between the garage and the kitchen. Strange, there was no welcoming bark from Perro, and the kitchen was in total darkness.

"Candy," she called, switching on the light. An instant later she was struck with dread.

The kitchen was in shambles. Cabinet and pantry doors hung open, revealing shelves ransacked and almost bare of the canned food and bottles of juice and soda they always kept on hand. On the table were the remains of a sketchy meal—crusts, crumbs, fragments of cold cuts, soda cans, and an empty container of chocolate ice cream.

Deirdre saw all this in that first fearful moment before she became aware of the frightening stillness.

"Candy!" she called again. She ran out of the kitchen, down the dark hallway to the living room. Switching on the light, she saw more evidence of ransacking and theft. But what chilled her heart was not the strewn contents of her desk nor the drawers of the highboy overturned on the floor, nor even the realization that her father's rifle was missing from its rack above the fireplace. The cold clutch of fear came from the sight of Candy's wheelchair standing empty near the hearth.

The door to the bedroom wing was closed. Trembling, she turned the knob, making her way into the hall, calling Candy's name. As she switched on the light, she heard the muffled sound of Perro barking. She threw open the door of the linen closet, and he bounded out. She hugged him, weeping, thankful he wasn't hurt.

Glancing down the hall, she saw that the door to Candy's room was closed. Perro reached it before she did and scratched at it and barked. She opened it to a dark room and before her shaky hands could find the light switch, she heard another sound—a kind of throaty moaning. Her heart leaped with hope.

"Candy?"

The light went on and there on the bed she saw Yolanda bound and gagged, but evidently unharmed. Candy must be in one of the other bedrooms, she thought with relief.

"Thank heaven you're all right, Yolanda," she said. She took the gag off Yolanda's mouth, then turned towards the door.

"I'll be right back to untie you, but first I have to see if Candy's all right too."

Yolanda's agitated voice filled Deirdre's heart with fresh fear.

"Candy's not here. They took her!"

Deirdre felt as though her entire being were paralyzed with dread. Somehow, her shaking hands began to unbind Yolanda and she managed to steady her voice.

"Tell me what happened."

Yolanda was almost hysterical. Her words poured out in a torrent.

"They came this morning soon after you left, Dee Dee. There were three of them . . ." She burst into sobs. "It's all my fault. I let them in. They knew your name. They were friends of Deirdre's, they said, come to pick up some shirts Deirdre's sister had for them. Perro barked at them when they came to the door, but one of the men called him by name. I thought it was all right to let them in. They wanted money and I only had about twenty dollars in my purse and Candy didn't have much more than that. They took my watch and Candy's too and all the jewelry that was your mother's. Why did they take her, Dee Dee? Did they kidnap her for ransom?"

She buried her face in her hands.

A sickening suspicion began to gnaw at Deirdre and mingle with the fear that Candy had indeed been taken for ransom.

Above the painful pounding of her heart, she heard a voice speaking calmly, and she realized it was her own voice, somehow able to come through her shock.

"It's not your fault, Yolanda. I'm going to call the police now, and when they come they're going to want a description of the men. Can you remember what they looked like?"

Yolanda nodded. She told Deirdre one man

was fat and had long, yellowish hair and one was black and bearded. They were in their mid-twenties, she thought. The third man was younger, short and stocky with dark hair, and looked like a Chicano.

"He's the one who knew Perro's name," Yolanda added.

Now the suspicion in Deirdre's mind burst into reality. There was no doubt, the youngest man was Herman.

She called the police, sick with the realization that Herman and the other two must have been planning an escape from the prison. Short of unlocking the gate for them, she'd given them everything they needed to facilitate the break-out. Once out, they needed a remote area to hide in until they could get food, money, and a car. Because of her stupidity, they knew the location of her house, knew it was surrounded by woods, and they had pictures of it, inside and out. They knew two women would be there, one in a wheel-chair, the other with a van they could steal. The picture of the fireplace had told them there'd be a gun ready for the taking, and they'd found ammunition in a chest drawer. She'd even provided them with Perro's name.

She pictured Candy lying gagged and helpless and terrified in the back of the van among the bottles and cans of stolen food. Had she been taken to ensure their getaway, or, as Yolanda had suggested, had she been kidnapped for ransom? Deirdre didn't know which possibility was the more frightening.

"We must look around and see if they left a ransom note," she said to Yolanda. They made a thorough search, but found nothing, and suddenly the calm she'd been able to maintain went to pieces and she found herself weeping as uncontrollably as she had after her parents' death. Yolanda tried to comfort her, but she too was so distraught that they found themselves weeping together.

Slowly, a thought made its way through her despair and told her what she needed to do. Still shaking with sobs, she picked up her purse from the floor where, in her agitation, she'd let it fall. She opened it and took out a scrap of paper. A moment later she called Gordon.

The police were already there and Deirdre had told the officer in charge the entire story about her involvement with Herman, when Gordon arrived. He didn't speak a word when he came in, but gathered her into his arms and held her there. She felt surrounded by warmth and comfort—like she did when she was a child in bed on a chilly night, and her mother would come and tuck an extra blanket around her.

Then Gordon extended his hand to the police officer.

"I'm Dr. Gordon Burns, Officer."

"Detective Tom Corbo. I take it you're the family physician."

Gordon cast Deirdre a glance. "In a way, yes. But I'm sure you know the young woman who was abducted is disabled and under the care of specialists."

The detective nodded, a grim look crossing his face. "Yes. This is one of the meanest cases I've ever come up against."

Gordon led Deirdre to the couch where Yolanda was huddled. He took a small case from his pocket. "I'm going to give each of you a sedative," he said. "And I also brought what I'll need to spend the night. Jake's covering my shift."

The officer rose from his chair and said he was going back to headquarters. He paused at the door and looked at Deirdre.

"I've made a full report. The FBI is being called in and everything possible is being done. I'll get back to you, but I left my number by the phone if you need to call me."

After he'd gone, Gordon brought water to Yolanda and Deirdre and handed them each a capsule.

"This is very mild, but it will calm you so you can get some sleep."

Deirdre stared at the capsule in her hand. She felt the beginning of yet another fear.

"I just thought of something—Candy's medication."

"Don't worry about that, Dee Dee," Yolanda said. "She has it with her."

"Oh Yolanda—are you sure?"

"Sure. She took a tablet a few minutes before those men came to the door and she put the bottle in her pocket till time for the next one."

Deirdre felt some of her anxiety ease, only to return full force a moment later. How could Candy take her medication if her hands were tied up and a gag put on her mouth?

Gordon must have had the same thought.

"Candy knows how necessary that medicine is. Let's not rule out the possibility that she'd find a way to let the men know and that they'd allow her to take it."

"The doctor's right, Dee Dee," Yolanda said. She took her sedative and said she was going to bed.

"I'll make up the guest room for the doctor before I turn in," she added. "I'll sleep in Candy's room."

Deirdre embraced her. "Thank you, Yolanda.

I hope you do get some sleep. You've had a terrible experience."

Yolanda seemed about to say something, but then closed her mouth firmly and went into the bedroom wing. Deirdre knew what she'd almost said—harrowing as her experience had been, it was over; but Candy's was only beginning.

Gordon seated himself beside her on the couch.

"Do you feel up to filling me in on the details?" he asked, and she realized that when she'd phoned him, she'd told him only that Candy had been abducted. She'd been too distraught to say any more.

"Detective Corbo says they're certain the men are three inmates reported escaped from the prison last night. It was assumed they were on foot and would head for the Mexican border, so sheriffs of border areas were alerted last night and extra patrols assigned. Now, of course, the search is being widened to the north."

Gordon frowned. "There was no connection between those men and Yolanda's van until you called the police and it was reported missing. They had almost a full day's start on the police and they know it. Valuable time was lost in assuming they were on foot, heading for the border." He paused, looking puzzled. "I don't understand how they happened to come here."

Deirdre felt a rush of tears. "I know why," she said. She choked back her sobs as she told him the whole story of Herman's betrayal.

"I feel so stupid!" she exclaimed. "I should have known what he was up to. Looking back at it now, I remember things he said. . . ."

"You mustn't blame yourself, Deirdre. There was no way you could have known what was going on."

She buried her face in his shoulder.

"Gordon—what's going to happen? Is Candy's life in danger?"

His hand stroked her hair. He kissed her gently on her brow and on her cheek, where a tear lingered.

"I'm not going to pretend I think everything's going to be all right. I'll tell you something, though—I'm not a religious man in the strict sense of the word, but I do believe in God, and I don't think God would have spared Candy's life in that accident, only to let it be taken now."

His words dulled the sharp daggers of fear that stabbed at her heart. She wondered if she'd ever find words to tell him how much he'd comforted her.

They went to their bedrooms soon afterward. Before she fell asleep, Deirdre breathed a prayer for Candy, and she knew without a doubt that down the hall in the guest room, the man who didn't consider himself religious was doing the same.

Chapter Eight

Deirdre was awakened the following morning by a gentle knock at her bedroom door. The sun's first rays were filtering through the blinds. Uneven shadows of the piñons outside her window danced on the wall opposite her bed, and her first thought was that it looked like the start of a beautiful day.

Then, with the full awakening of her senses, she remembered.

"Dee Dee?" Yolanda's voice pulled her further back to reality. She breathed a deep sigh and answered.

"Come in, Yolanda."

"I've brought breakfast," Yolanda said. "Those creeps didn't leave us much, but I managed to put something together. Now don't tell me you're not hungry. You've got to eat. You'll need your strength."

Yolanda seemed to have found her own strength, Deirdre thought. She was her old self again. She poured coffee from a small china pot and handed the cup and saucer to Deirdre.

"The doctor was up early and made the coffee. He's taking a shower now and he said he'd look in on you before he left."

She glanced at the television set. "The morning paper hasn't come yet, but the news should be on. Do you want to look at it?"

"I suppose we should."

Just as she had anticipated, the story of Candy's abduction was all over the news, with commentators speculating whether or not a ransom demand would be made.

Yolanda hastened to switch it off, just as a commentator started to evaluate Candy's chances of being released alive.

"What does he know?" she said. "Finish your breakfast and go have your bath, Dee Dee."

When Deirdre emerged from her bathroom, swathed in her robe, with her wet hair bundled under a towel, Gordon knocked at her bedroom door. She let him in.

"Excuse me," he said with a grin. "I've got to

get to the hospital. I didn't want to leave without seeing you."

Yolanda had been making up the bed. Now Deirdre saw her mouth twitch into a smile as she plumped up the pillows and arranged the spread.

"Well, Dr. Burns, you're seeing me as I really am," Deirdre replied, smiling ruefully and adjusting the oversized turban on her head. It was good to make light talk for a minute or two.

He took her hands and looked searchingly into her eyes.

"Will you be okay?"

Yolanda answered for her. "Sure, she'll be okay, Doctor. I'll be here with her."

Gordon cast her a smile. "I'm counting on you to see that she behaves herself, Yolanda." He looked at Deirdre again. "I'll get back here as soon as I can. I'll phone you later."

She was enveloped in a brief, strong embrace and felt the touch of a kiss on her cheek, and then he was gone.

With the morning under way, the telephone began to ring.

Despite Yolanda's protests, Deirdre insisted on taking the calls. It would keep the fear and the worry from getting the best of her, she told herself.

Besides, the number was unlisted. She knew the calls would be from those who truly cared. She was right. Friends and neighbors phoned, and Mr. Gillespie and some shopowners from Old Town, to let her know Candy was in their thoughts and prayers.

"I must call Grandmother and Grandpa before this news gets to Florida," she told Yolanda.

"Don't wait too long. This is the kind of news that goes out all over the country pretty quick," Yolanda replied.

Before she had a chance to pick up the phone, a steady stream of caring people began coming to the house, some bringing casseroles and platters of food, others offering to stay with her if Yolanda needed to go home.

Tom Corbo called to give her some background information on the three men.

"None of them is considered dangerous. Bear in mind, they could have killed your sister and your housekeeper, but didn't."

Instead, they only abducted a helpless, disabled woman, Deirdre thought angrily. She wanted to say she considered three men with a loaded rifle dangerous, especially the one Herman had told her had shot the owner of the liquor store. But she knew the detective was only trying to calm her fears. He was a decent, compassionate man with a dirty job to do.

"Do you know yet how they escaped?" she asked.

"Yes, we've determined that," Corbo replied. "They hid in the back of an exterminator's truck. They knew the exterminator came regularly once a month. They knew the truck would be driven to Albuquerque when the job was done and from the lettering on the truck, they knew exactly where—an address on southeast Central—not too long a hike to the foothills."

Deirdre wondered how Herman and his cohorts could have left the cell area, reached the service yard, and slipped into the back of a truck, unnoticed by guards. When she turned on the television again, she discovered she wasn't the only one with such questions. Outraged individuals and civic organizations were charging prison officials with lax security and corruption and calling for a complete overhaul of the penal system.

She was picking at a plate of lunch Yolanda had insisted on preparing, when her grandfather phoned. With a pang of guilt, she realized she'd forgotten to call him.

He told her the news about Candy had just come on television.

"Your grandmother is so upset, she can't even come to the phone," he said. Deirdre heard his voice choke up. "Are you all right, honey? Who's with you?"

"Yolanda's here, and friends and neighbors have been in and out. Don't worry about *me,* Grandpa. Just pray that Candy will get through this unharmed."

She heard Grandmother's voice in the background, high-pitched and tearful. Grandpa came on again.

"Your grandmother wants to know if we should fly out there and be with you, Deirdre. We can get a flight out this afternoon. What do you think, honey?"

Deirdre hesitated. Her grandparents were the only family she and Candy had, and they wanted to close ranks at this terrible time. But with Grandmother too distraught even to talk on the phone....

"Having you here would be a great comfort, Grandpa—but do you think Grandmother is up to it?"

"No, honey, not right now she isn't. I guess we'd better give her a chance to calm down. I'll call you tomorrow."

Tomorrow. The word echoed in Deirdre's mind long after she hung up the phone. Would there be a tomorrow for Candy? She wanted to cry again, but now her despair was so deep she felt as if she had no more tears left to shed.

Yolanda came out of the kitchen and eyed the lunch plate disapprovingly.

"Mrs. Trujillo made those fajitas especially for you, Dee Dee, and you didn't take more than two bites."

"I know—I just don't feel like eating." She sighed. "Everyone has been so thoughtful and you've been so good to me, Yolanda. You should be thinking about getting home soon, though. You have your husband to think of. My friend Nancy said she'd come and stay this afternoon if I needed her."

"I promised the doctor I'd look after you," Yolanda said. "Besides, Lupe won't be back from his hunting trip till tonight. I'll phone him later."

Not long afterwards Yolanda picked up the ringing phone.

"Speak of the devil," she said to Deirdre. "It's Lupe." Then Deirdre saw her eyes widen and her face grow grave. For several minutes Yolanda listened intently and said nothing until her "good-bye" ended the conversation. Her face, as she turned to Deirdre, was agitated.

"What is it, Yolanda? What happened?" Deirdre's mind was suddenly filled with thoughts of a hunting accident.

"They saw the van, Dee Dee—Lupe and his friends—last night when they stopped to eat in a town up near the Jemez. Lupe thought it was me, but the van took off before he could see the license or who was in it."

Deirdre was stunned, speechless.

"They all decided it couldn't have been our van, but this morning they turned on the radio in the camper and heard the news about Candy. They came right back to Albuquerque and went straight to the police. That's where Lupe was calling from."

Deirdre felt her stomach churning. The police now knew where Candy and her captors had been last night.

"That's good news, Yolanda," she said.

"Lupe's going back to the pueblo and round up a posse to help the police search the Jemez," Yolanda said.

The phone rang again. Tom Corbo was on the line, and from the sound of his voice, Deirdre sensed trouble.

"Officer Corbo—Yolanda's husband told us about sighting the van," she said. "That's good news, isn't it—knowing the general location?"

His hesitation in replying sent a stab of apprehension into her heart.

"Yes, of course that's helpful. But there's been a new development. A clerk at an Albuquerque post office found an unstamped envelope while he was sorting mail this morning. He tossed it aside because it had no stamp. Later, he looked at it again and saw it was addressed to 'Dedra Lane, care of the Albuquerque Police Department.' He's just brought it in to us and I've opened it."

Deirdre's heart gave a lurch. "It's a ransom note, isn't it?"

"Yes. An FBI agent is on her way out to your place now."

She was in a daze as she replaced the phone. A moment later she realized he hadn't told her how much money was demanded. But it didn't matter; she'd give every dollar she had to get Candy back.

By two o'clock that afternoon, procedures had been set in motion. An FBI agent, Lisa Palmer, had been stationed in the house. Another agent had accompanied Deirdre to her bank, where she'd withdrawn sixty-five thousand dollars from her money-market account and cashed in two certificates of deposit. Then they'd gone to her stockbroker, an old friend of her father's, who facilitated the sale of securities to make up the total amount demanded—one hundred thousand dollars.

When Deirdre was shown the ransom note, she could barely read it. It was a jumble of misspelled and crossed-out words specifying where the money was to be left, and warning her not to call the police. If she hadn't been so distraught she would have found this warning amusing, since the note had been sent to the police station. Obviously, Herman and his friends had enough smarts to plan a slick escape but had trouble putting together the rest of it. The location where the money was to be left had been crossed out and changed from "behind the big rock on the road" to "under the bridge" and again to "near the door of the Catholic church in Jemez Springs at eight o'clock Tuesday night." It seemed to her that they weren't sure of what they were doing.

She mentioned this to Agent Palmer, who commented tersely, "They're not the sharpest group I've ever dealt with."

This gave rise to a new fear. Uncertainty could lead to blunders resulting in panic. She'd been told that none of Candy's captors had ever killed anyone, but panic could cause unpredictable reactions.

She was also uneasy that instead of herself, a policewoman was to deliver the ransom money to the specified place. But the police assured her that this was the best way to handle it.

When she returned home from the bank, Yolanda told her that Gordon had phoned and said he'd be there around six that evening. She smiled and added, "I like the doctor, Dee Dee."

It was no secret that Yolanda had never liked Paul. Even before the breakup she'd insisted his black hair and dark eyes indicated he was Hispanic, and that his real name must be Martinez, not Martin. Yolanda believed he'd changed his name and turned his back on his true heritage.

"The doctor asked me was I taking good care of you," Yolanda said. She gave Deirdre a penetrating look. "You look beat. You better go take a nap."

"I couldn't sleep, Yolanda. My mind's in a turmoil. Besides, they might call me from police headquarters."

"I'll wake you up if they do. Go on now. I'll bring you a cup of herb tea; that'll relax you."

Deirdre went into her bedroom, took off her shoes, and lay down on the bed. Thoughts of Candy filled her mind. Had she been able to take her medicine? Had she been warm enough last night? Yolanda had said she'd only been wearing a light jacket. Had they given her anything to eat? Had they mistreated her? She forced herself to blot out the next thought. It was too terrible to contemplate.

"Now drink this," Yolanda said as she came into the room with the tea. She sat down on the side of the bed. "Everything's in the works now,

Dee Dee. Those FBI people know what they're doing. All we have to do is wait now."

Deirdre drank the tea and lay back on the pillows, hazily aware of Yolanda covering her with a quilt. She told herself she'd catch a few winks—just enough so she wouldn't be too exhausted when Gordon arrived.

The room was full of shadows when she awoke to the sound of Perro barking. A few minutes later she heard Yolanda talking to someone in the hallway. Gordon? A glance at her watch told her it was half past five. Gordon must have been able to get away from the hospital early.

She swung her legs over the side of the bed and put on her shoes, just as a knock came at the door.

"Dee, it's me, Paul."

She opened the door and he came in, followed by a visibly annoyed Yolanda.

"It's all right, Yolanda," she said. She looked at Paul. He'd come to console her. If she couldn't be gracious, she must at least be civil.

"It was very nice of you to come, Paul."

"I couldn't believe it at first," he said. "And on the way out here I heard on my radio that there'd been a ransom demand."

"Yes, there was."

He shook his head. "That's rough. Is there anything I can do?"

"No—but thanks for asking."

"Is it true they're demanding a hundred thousand?"

"That's right."

He gave a low whistle. "Were you able to come up with that kind of money on such short notice on your own?"

She wanted to ask him if he were there to express his concern or to explore her financial status. Instead, she swallowed hard on the words and changed the subject.

"Paul, I've just awakened from a nap and I want to freshen up."

She hoped he'd tell her he had to be going.

"I'll wait for you in the living room," he said.

When she joined him, he glanced at her appraisingly.

"You're looking good, Dee. With everything that's happened, I thought you'd be a wreck."

Indignation seethed inside her. He hadn't the slightest inkling of how devastated she was.

Yolanda came out of the kitchen. She spoke directly to Deirdre, but stole a slightly belligerent glance at Paul.

"A car just came into the drive. It might be the doctor. He said he'd be here around this time."

Paul stared at her, then at Deirdre. "You called the doctor? Well, I guess with the strain you've been under, you do need a good tranquilizer."

When the doorbell sounded. Perro bounded towards the door, barking and snarling, then quieted down as soon as Yolanda let Gordon in.

Deirdre sprang to her feet. Paul's presence was not going to keep her from hurrying to greet Gordon. Had it only been this morning since she'd seen him last? It seemed an eternity.

If Gordon noticed Paul sitting on the couch, it didn't stop him from enfolding her in his arms.

"I'm glad you're here," she whispered.

She turned towards the couch, where Paul was eyeing Gordon with surprise and displeasure.

"You two met in the shop—remember?" she asked.

Gordon nodded. Before he could reply, Paul spoke.

"Yes, I've met the cowboy." He got to his feet and said he had to be running along.

"Take care of yourself, Dee," he said. "When the doctor comes, be sure and get those tranquilizers. Shelling out all that money must have really done a number on your nerves."

The door closed behind him.

"I wish you'd had a chance to tell him you're the doctor we were expecting," she told Gordon.

"I couldn't care less what that jerk thinks. Did he upset you, Deirdre?"

"No." It was true. Paul's insensitivity had lost much of its power to affect her.

"But in the past there was something, wasn't there? When are you going to tell me about it?"

A moment later he was leading her to the couch, drawing her down beside him.

"I take back the question. I shouldn't be badgering you at a time like this. It's going to be a rough night."

"How long can you stay?"

"As long as you need me."

"Did Jake change hours with you again?"

"Yes, and several others volunteered. Everyone wants you to know they're thinking about you and pulling for Candy."

"I'm scared, Gordon," she said.

He put his arms around her and drew her close. "Of course you are."

"Agent Palmer as much as said they were the dumbest kidnappers she'd ever come up against. I can't help thinking—suppose they're dumb enough to bungle the whole thing? They could panic and . . ." She began to tremble.

His arms tightened around her.

"Try not to think like that. I'm sure the police and the FBI have taken that into consideration. They have all bases covered, Deirdre." He kissed her brow. "Let's listen to some music for a while. Later, there's an old Clark Gable picture on the movie channel."

She knew he was right. While they waited through the hours to come, she must try to get her mind off what might be happening.

Chapter Nine

Agent Palmer had turned the den into a communications center.

When it was time for the movie to start, Gordon moved the television set into the living room and Yolanda brought their dinner to them on trays, then turned and headed back to the kitchen.

"Aren't you going to watch Clark Gable with us?" Deirdre asked.

Yolanda shook her head. "I'm going to make a batch of Candy's favorite piñon cookes."

Deirdre wished she could share Yolanda's hopes that Candy would be home soon. But however hard she tried, her own doubts dragged her back into deep pessimism.

135

When the clock on the mantel struck eight, she was reminded that the ransom money should now be in place at the church door. Two separate scenarios whirled about in her mind— one in which the money was picked up and Candy released unharmed, the other in which her worst fears were realized.

Deirdre glanced through the door to the study where Agent Palmer was talking on the phone.

"She'll get word right away, won't she?" she asked Gordon.

"Palmer? Sure."

She buried her face in his shoulder. "I don't know what I'd do, if . . ."

He put his arms around her and held her close, and she knew that whatever happened, whether it were to rejoice or to mourn, he'd be there for her. In his arms she would always find what she needed—joy, contentment, solace, comfort.

Deep inside her a feeling unlike any other she'd known started to grow, and before she recognized it for what it was, it had taken over her heart and mind. Then she knew it was the love she'd been thrusting away, telling herself she couldn't risk having it, denying it, even after he'd told her what was in his own heart. Now it was too strong to be denied—more powerful than she'd ever believed a love could be.

She felt herself trembling and knew the time

had come to tell him what he'd been waiting to hear, ever since that evening in the observatory.

As though he'd sensed something, he cupped her chin in his hand and raised her face, looking into her eyes.

"What is it, Deirdre?"

"Oh, Gordon—I think you know!"

"I only know what I hope, dearest. Tell me."

She told him, speaking the three small words almost breathlessly. She watched a light come into his eyes, and then she felt his lips on hers in the kiss they'd been waiting so long to share.

He smiled into her eyes.

"I was beginning to wonder if I'd ever hear you say it. I think I've loved you ever since I first saw you outside your shop that morning."

Something in his eyes, something in his voice, told her he was waiting for her to tell him what had happened with Paul. But telling him would serve no purpose. It was over. He would only be hurt to know that the bitterness she'd felt towards another man had been keeping them apart.

"Ms. Lane?" The F.B.I. agent was standing in the study doorway.

She was jolted back to grim reality. "Has there been any word?" she asked.

"Only that the money hasn't been picked up yet."

The now-familiar daggers began to stab at her heart again.

"It's not even eight-thirty," Gordon said. She knew he was trying to allay her fears. But until the money was picked up and a note left in its place with instructions leading to Candy, things were at a standstill.

"Suppose they don't pick up the money?" she asked.

"It's too soon to speculate on that," Agent Palmer said, and then went back to the telephone.

"You've stationed men all around that church, haven't you?" Deirdre called after her. She heard her own voice growing shrill with fear and anger. "You've scared them away!"

Gordon got to his feet and went into the study, where he talked quietly with the agent. Returning, he took Deirdre's hands in his.

"There will be no move to apprehend the kidnappers until Candy is safe. According to the ransom note, whoever picks up the money will leave a note directing the agents to another place where there'll be another note telling where Candy can be found. There'll be plenty of time to get back to the van and let Candy go before they take off with the money."

She clung to him, trying to choke back her sobs. She thought about Herman and couldn't keep the tears from rising and spilling over her cheeks. She remembered how pleased he'd been with the shirt Candy had painted. How could he do such a terrible thing to a helpless young woman who'd tried to bring a little pleasure into his life? How could he return her own kindness with such cruelty?

"Cry as much as you need to, dearest," Gordon said. "Don't try to talk."

She laid her head upon his shoulder and listened to the clock ticking away the minutes, resounding almost painfully in her ears. She heard the chime of the quarter hour telling her it would soon be nine o'clock.

Through the study door, she could see the FBI agent talking on the phone. She was sure Agent Palmer's face looked even more grim than it had earlier.

"Something's gone wrong, Gordon," she whispered. She was too gripped with fear to weep any more.

He made no reply, but only tightened his arms around her.

"I should have been the one to leave the money," she said. "That's why it hasn't been picked up."

"Deirdre, sweetheart, assuming it was going to be Herman who picked up the money—and assuming he was somewhere in the vicinity, watching—in the darkness and at a distance, there'd be no way he could tell it wasn't you."

"I should have gone up there," she insisted. "Maybe if I could have talked to Herman...."

Her voice trailed off. She was being irrational and Gordon had every right to tell her so. Instead, he kissed her gently.

"I agree with the way the police and the FBI are handling it. It wouldn't have accomplished anything to have you make the trip up to the Jemez. It would only have caused you more strain."

Yolanda came out of the kitchen with some cookies on a plate.

"You might as well eat a few of these while we're waiting for Candy." She glanced towards the television set. "How's the movie?"

Deirdre realized they hadn't been watching it at all.

"Has there been any word?" Yolanda asked.

Deirdre shook her head. "Nobody picked up the money yet."

Yolanda put the plate of cookies on a nearby table and went back into the kitchen.

She's just as fearful as I am, Deirdre thought.

She rested her head on Gordon's shoulder and closed her eyes.

* * *

"I'm sorry," she said. She'd opened her eyes and realized she'd been asleep in Gordon's arms.

"Don't apologize. I enjoyed watching you snooze. Do you know you have very long eyelashes?"

"I hope you like long eyelashes. What time is it?"

When he hesitated, she turned towards the clock and saw it was ten fifteen. She looked questioningly at him.

"Was there any word while I was sleeping?"

"Nothing new. A few minutes ago, the agent signaled me that nobody had picked up the money yet."

Again, daggers were at her heart.

"Gordon—will you tell me, truthfully, what you think is happening?"

He cast her a long look and she saw some of her own fears in his eyes.

"All right, I'll level with you." He held her close to him and she could feel his heart drumming with hers. "I think you were right on the mark when you said those men might panic. I think that's what's happened, dearest."

"And—Candy?"

"I don't know. . . ." He seemed to be searching for further words. "They could have released her somewhere and taken off."

The thought of Candy put out of the van, perhaps lying helpless in the dark somewhere, was frightening, but it was the least frightening of all the other thoughts which crowded her mind. She found herself clinging to it as though it were a floating log keeping her from being swept away in turbulent waters.

Agent Palmer had come to the study door again.

"We're not waiting any longer for the money to be picked up. A search of the area surrounding Jemez Springs has been ordered."

She added that roadblocks had been set up since early afternoon on all possible routes north out of Jemez Springs.

Yolanda came out of the kitchen just in time to hear this.

"That's good," she said. "There wouldn't be any chance of that old van getting through without being searched."

Deirdre knew what she meant. Yolanda had given a detailed description to the police. They knew the van was an old solid-sided Ford, plain white, except for a large Zia symbol Lupe had painted on the rear door. This Indian symbol of the sun made the van unique.

She began to sort everything out in her mind. Knowing that the kidnappers would not risk going south, the police had set up roadblocks north of the Jemez area. The kidnappers would have been caught by now if they'd tried to drive out of the area. That meant they were still in the vicinity.

The agent was looking at Deirdre with an expression of mingled gravity and compassion.

"I've been asked to prepare you, Ms. Lane. Even when the van is apprehended or found somewhere around the Jemez, it doesn't look good for your sister."

Her heart was a leaden weight. She heard her own voice, sounding as though it were coming from afar.

"Thank you for telling me. I don't want to keep going on false hopes."

"I'm not saying there's no hope, Ms. Lane," Agent Palmer said. She went back into the study.

Gordon took Deirdre's hands in his. "She's right, sweetheart."

"Hope and prayer—that's all Candy has going for her now," Deirdre said. She rested her head against his chest. "Oh Gordon, she was such a dear person—so lively—so funny...."

She was shocked by her own words. She was talking about Candy as though she were dead!

Gordon was stroking her hair, smoothing it with the gentleness so much a part of him.

"Do you remember what I told you—how I didn't believe God would spare Candy's life in the accident, then allow her to die in a kidnapping?" he asked.

She raised her head and looked into his eyes. "Yes, I remember. It comforted me then and it comforts me now."

They sat in silence, arms entwined, and she thought of the many times Candy had tried to bring them together. She took further comfort in knowing that Candy had seen in Gordon everything she, herself, had been too embittered to recognize. If only Candy could know about her change of heart.

She was so deep in thought, she only half heard the agent speaking her name.

"Ms. Lane—"

When Deirdre turned to look at her she saw a smile on her face.

"Your sister is safe and sound at Albuquerque police headquarters," Agent Palmer said. "One of the kidnappers brought her in a few minutes ago and gave himself up—he said his name is Herman."

Chapter Ten

Deirdre felt as though she were caught up in a whirlwind of joy.

The minute she heard those incredible words, her heart came unbound from its fetters of fear. She found herself laughing, and then crying tears of relief. She threw her arms around Gordon and kissed him, then embraced Yolanda, then hugged each of them again in a round of sheer jubilation which even included a hug for the FBI agent.

"We'll have your sister brought home as soon as her statement has been taken," Agent Palmer told her when things began to quiet down.

"I don't want to wait," she said. "I want to go

down to the police station now—but first I must call our grandparents."

"And while we're downtown, I'd like to take Candy over to the hospital and make sure she's okay," Gordon added. "Go ahead and make your call, Deirdre, then we'll go."

The call was very brief, but she knew its message couldn't have caused more joy if she'd talked for an hour.

Gordon was folding Candy's wheelchair. "Are we all set? Come on, Deirdre—you too, Yolanda, let's go!"

"All right," the agent said. "I'll call headquarters and tell them you're on your way. I'll stay here. I'm waiting for word about the other two men."

Deirdre grabbed an afghan and a pillow from the couch and Gordon took the wheelchair. They hurried out to his car, followed by Yolanda, who clutched a sack of piñon cookies.

The road winding down from the foothills had never been as swiftly traveled, Deirdre was sure. On the highway, Gordon happily ignored the speed limit.

"There isn't a cop in the state who'd give me a ticket tonight!" he said.

They pulled up outside the police station in record time. Deirdre was out of the car almost before Gordon hit the brakes, and while she was running into the station house she found herself wondering if this could be a euphoric dream from which she'd awaken to grim reality.

It wasn't until she was holding Candy close to her and letting their happy tears blend, that she knew it was true. Dear Candy was safe and unharmed and seemed surprisingly unaffected by her ordeal.

Tom Corbo, who'd greeted them in the hall, told them Candy had given her statement and was ready to go.

They lifted her out of the chair in the chief's office into her wheelchair, put the pillow at her back, and tucked the afghan around her. Yolanda thrust the sack of cookies into her hand.

"All this and piñon cookies too!" Candy exclaimed. "If I'd known I was going to get this royal treatment, I'd have arranged to be kidnapped long before this!"

She took Deirdre's hand. "Dee Dee, I owe my life to Herman."

Deirdre felt a rush of conflicting emotions—first anger, then gratitude.

"Where is he, Candy? Did they send him back to the prison?"

"No. He's here in a holding cell. The detective said he hasn't spoken a word since he gave himself up, except to say he wants to see you."

Tom Corbo had been standing nearby. "That's

right. He refuses to give us any kind of statement. It would be helpful if you'd agree to let me take you to see him. Maybe he'll talk to you."

Deirdre knew she must go. Angry as she was, she had to let Herman know she was thankful that he'd brought Candy back. She consulted with Gordon, who told her he'd take Candy to the hospital for a checkup and come back to the station house for her afterwards.

"I'll take Yolanda with us," he said. "We won't be long." He kissed her and held her in his arms for a moment, before Deirdre turned to go with Tom Corbo.

When she glanced over her shoulder for another look at Candy, she knew Gordon's kiss and tender embrace had not gone unobserved. Candy was smiling. It was the kind of smile that happens when a fervent wish comes true.

Herman was huddled on a cot in a corner of the cell, his back turned. When Tom Corbo spoke his name, he looked up. When he saw Deirdre, he got to his feet, came to the gate, and reached through the bars as if he wanted desperately to touch her.

"I wish I hadn't done it," he said.

She looked into the eyes of the man who'd caused her so much anguish, and felt only compassion.

"It's all right now, Herman. You brought her back to me unharmed." She paused to take his hand in hers. "Will you tell me what happened?"

With Tom Corbo standing nearby, recording every word, Herman began to talk.

He told of spending the night in the woods near the house, waiting till they saw Deirdre leave for work in the morning. Then they went in. They'd figured it all out. It would be dark before she came home and discovered what had happened. They had all day to carry out their plan without fear of apprehension. The abduction of Candy and the theft of Yolanda's van wouldn't be reported until hours later.

"We thought it was a good joke, them looking for us down around El Paso and thinking we didn't even have a car," Herman said.

He described how they'd tied Candy's hands behind her back, put a gag on her mouth, and stretched her out in the back of the van. When they started off, he was riding in the back with her and he went through her pockets, thinking she might have some money there.

"We had to gas up the van and buy some stuff, and we didn't have much cash. But she didn't have none. All I found was a bottle of pills. I asked her did she have to take one soon and she nodded her head yes. I told her to let me know when it was time, and I'd untie the gag and she could take the pill with some soda."

They'd stopped for gas in a town on the way to the Jemez and bought cans of red and black spray paint, and they'd stolen a license plate from a car there. That must have been where Lupe and his friends had seen the van, Deirdre thought.

When they reached the mountains they drove the van into the woods and sprayed black paint over the rear door to hide the Zia symbol, then sprayed red-and-black stripes along the sides. They put the stolen license plate on and threw Yolanda's into a gully.

"Leo said now we could go all the way to Canada without nobody stopping us, but we had to get the money first."

He told how they'd planned to telephone their ransom demand, but Deirdre's number was unlisted. And they didn't know the house address.

"Leo said we should have gotten the number off your phone while we was in the house, but nobody thought of it, so we wrote that letter to the police. We was sure you'd get it even if it didn't have a stamp. We didn't have no stamps on us and the post office was closed."

He said he began to feel uneasy when they couldn't agree where Candy should be released.

"Leo and Vinny was talking like they'd leave

her somewheres in the woods that night after we got the money. They didn't want her to be found too quick. I didn't like that, not with her being a cripple and all."

They spent the night in the woods. The next day they heard news of the kidnapping on the radio and learned that the FBI was on the case.

"Vinny said that when the FBI was in on it that it meant the death penalty. Leo started hollering at him, and I could tell they was both getting scared."

They argued all day about who was to pick up the money.

"Leo said nobody would touch the one who picked it up because they wanted Candy back alive. Then they told me I had to do it, but I said no—I was the one got us the van and the girl, and we already agreed I didn't have to do it. While we was fighting about it, it got to be time to pick up the money. Then Leo said why didn't we forget the money and drive up north somewheres where we could rip off some stores. Vinny said yeah, nobody would stop us with the van looking so different. I could tell that's what they was going to do."

They first agreed that Candy would be released near the roadside that night and given a flashlight. But then Leo pointed out that Candy had seen the cans of paint when they were put in the back of the van. She knew they'd painted the van red and black and would tell the police.

"I knew right then your sister didn't have a chance. Leo never killed nobody before, but he was scared now and so was Vinny. Leo said we had to get rid of her. I didn't know what to do. Vinny does what Leo says, so it was two against one. There was a shovel and pick in the back of the van, and Leo said we should start digging a hole to hide her in right after we shot her. We had to get out of there fast."

While they were digging they talked about who should do the shooting.

"Then I got this idea. I said I'd do it, and when we was almost done digging I took the gun out of the front of the van and walked around to the back like I was going to take your sister out. But I kept going around to the driver's side and jumped in quick and drove off."

Herman kept going until he reached the main road before he stopped the van and untied Candy and took the gag out of her mouth.

"I told her not to be scared. She'd be with her sister in a couple of hours."

Then he drove directly to the Albuquerque police station.

"What's going to happen to him now? Will he be returned to prison?" Deirdre asked Tom

Corbo. She'd come close to tears when she'd pressed Herman's hand and said good-bye.

"I can't say for sure," Corbo replied.

In the chief's office they were told that Herman's two cohorts had been tracked and captured in the Jemez by a posse of men from the Santo Domingo pueblo who were working with the police.

Deirdre's first feeling of satisfaction was overshadowed by another thought. When Herman and the other two were all returned to prison, would there be reprisals against Herman for turning against them?

"Can't Herman be put in some other prison?" she asked Tom Corbo and the chief. She could tell they understood what she meant.

"We're putting him in the jail downtown for a while," the chief said. "Under the unusual circumstances, there'll be a hearing to decide where he'll be sent or if leniency is in order."

"I want to be at the hearing," Deirdre said.

At that moment, Gordon came in to say that Candy had suffered no ill effects from her ordeal, other than fatigue.

"She and Yolanda are waiting in the car. We should get her home and to bed as soon as possible. Are we all finished here?" he asked.

"All done," Tom Corbo said. He turned to Deirdre. "We'll see that you're escorted to the

bank tomorrow to put your money back. Everything will be returned as quickly as possible—
the gun, the jewelry found in the van, and the
van itself. I'll let you know when Herman's hearing is scheduled."

Chapter Eleven

"When is all this hoopla about my kidnapping going to stop?" Candy asked Deirdre. "It's been almost a week and the story's still on the front page."

They were eating breakfast and reading the morning paper, which featured a picture of Herman with an item saying his hearing was scheduled for the following day.

"Don't hold your breath," Deirdre replied. "The idea of a kidnapper bringing his victim to the police station and turning himself in is something people can't get enough of. The story's big everywhere. When I talked to Grandpa yesterday, he said it's still all over the news in Florida."

155

Candy glanced back at the newspaper. "What do you think's going to happen at the hearing? Will Herman be paroled?"

"I hope so. I'm going to speak up for him at the hearing. And of course Tom Corbo will have his statement on tape. I hope the judge will be convinced that Herman deserves some leniency—but it's such a strange situation."

"Dee Dee, I know you don't want me to, but I'm definitely going to the hearing with you. If anyone could convince the judge that Herman deserves leniency, I could."

"Oh, Candy." Deirdre shook her head and sighed. "You've been through such a traumatic experience; I don't think you should go. It would only mean more publicity and you just told me you wanted it all to end."

"Maybe they'll take photos of me at the hearing," Candy said with a grin. "Looking at my face on the front page would be enough to turn everybody off, coast to coast."

Deirdre laughed, along with Candy, but beneath the laughter was the hope that Candy wouldn't have to joke about her face after the next surgery. It was scheduled for the following week.

The phone rang and Deirdre jumped to answer it. She knew it would be Gordon. He'd been calling every day. They hadn't seen much of each other since the night Candy came home. He was paying Jake and the others back for the hours they'd switched during the crisis. And with the shop closed for a few days, they hadn't even had brief visits in Old Town.

The sound of his voice filled her with joy. Now that she'd opened up her heart to him, she could savor the pure happiness of being in love.

"I miss you like crazy," he said. "We haven't had a chance to talk about *us* since you broke down and said those three little words."

"I miss you too. When do you think we can have some time together?"

"It looks good for tomorrow night."

"Come for dinner," she said. "We'll have a lot to talk about, not only about us but about Herman's hearing. It's set for tomorrow morning."

"And you're going up to bat for him."

"Yes, and so is Candy. I couldn't talk her out of it."

"With you two on his side, there's sure to be some leniency. Maybe he'll get parole. See you tomorrow night, sweetheart. I love you."

"Oh, Gordon, I love you too, with all my heart," she said. She knew no truer words had ever been spoken.

The next morning, when Yolanda was told Gordon was coming for dinner, she started baking an apple pie and said she'd make her chicken with green chiles and rice before she went home.

"All you'll have to do is make a salad," she added.

Deirdre gave her a hug. She knew Yolanda had been upset all week about the red-and-black paint sprayed on her van. Because of the deductible, her auto insurance wouldn't cover repainting.

"I know that old van's no Rolls Royce, but it's all I have and I hate driving around with it looking like a circus wagon," she'd said.

Deirdre had already told Yolanda she'd pay for having the van repainted, but Yolanda's reaction was no surprise. She was a proud woman who turned down offers of financial help.

Dinner that night was a celebration. Deirdre set the table in the dining room instead of the kitchen and brought out the fine china, silverware, and crystal candelabra their mother had always used for special occasions.

The finishing touch was the bouquet of red roses Gordon placed in her hands when she opened the door.

"This has been an incredible day," she said after they'd kissed and lingered for a moment in each other's arms. "And now that you're here, it's perfect."

"I heard a brief news report about Herman's hearing. Is it true that he was pardoned?"

"Yes—it's almost unbelievable, isn't it?"

"Very surprising. I thought he might get parole, but a pardon.... You and Candy must really have impressed the judge."

"We can't take full credit," Candy said as she wheeled out of the dining room. "Like Dee Dee said, it was almost unbelievable. Tell him, Dee Dee, but make it quick. Dinner's almost ready."

She wheeled back to the dining room to light the candles.

"Don't keep me in suspense," Gordon said. "What happened at the hearing?"

He drew her onto the couch, and she snuggled into his arms and began to tell him.

"There weren't many people at the hearing— just Candy and I, some news reporters, prison officials and police, and of course Herman and the judge.

"After Tom Corbo played the tape of what Herman told me, the judge listened to what Candy and I had to say. He seemed very moved by Candy's plea for leniency, and I was sure he was going to grant Herman a parole. But he didn't. Instead, he said he would only release him on parole if there were some responsible friend or relative he could live with, or at least close to. Otherwise, the best he could do for him was to assign him to the honor farm, where the men can go out to jobs each day but are expected to return in the evening. Herman has no family and the only friends he has are those two punks."

"Maybe the judge thought you and Candy would volunteer to be responsible for him," Gordon put in.

"If he did, he was mistaken. We're both grateful to Herman, but neither of us can forget what he did and how it might have turned out," Deirdre said.

"Then what happened?"

"The judge was about to sentence Herman to the honor farm, saying it was a privilege to be there and that Herman had earned the privilege. He described it and made it sound like anything but a prison, which it really is, no matter what they call it. In the middle of this, a young woman burst into the room, followed by a man. The woman was so good-looking and so beautifully dressed and the man had such an air of authority about him that everyone was staring at them, even the judge.

"Then, before anyone realized what was happening, the young woman was calling 'Hermano, Hermano!' and then she and Herman were hugging and kissing each other and the room was buzzing with excitement and the judge was banging his gavel and calling the hearing back to order."

"Who was this woman?" Gordon asked.

"His sister, Rita. He'd told me about her. They lost track of each other after they were placed in separate foster homes six years ago."

"How could that happen?"

"From what she told the judge, they lost contact soon after they were separated. Herman was moved around from foster home to foster home and Rita couldn't keep up with him."

"That sounds like the system was fouled up, somewhere."

"I guess so. Anyway, Rita was adopted and taken out of state. She said her adoptive parents made every effort to help her locate Herman, but without success. Meanwhile, Rita had a very good life. Her adoptive parents were wealthy. She was sent to private school, then to college, and last year she was married."

"I take it the authoritative-looking man who came to the hearing with her is her husband."

"Right. He provided the judge with all kinds of documents. I couldn't help but notice that the judge seemed very impressed with them."

"I can see the picture developing. With a long-lost sister showing up, Herman now has family. That would get him parole, but I don't understand how it would get him a pardon, unless of course, his sister lived in the White House."

"You've got the general idea. Rita's husband happens to be very close to someone who *does* live in the White House."

Gordon gave a whistle. "That certainly is some story," he said. "I wonder why the media didn't pick up on it. All I heard on the news was that Herman had been pardoned."

"The judge cleared the room of all spectators except Candy and me before he examined Rita's documents. When he announced the pardon to the press, nothing was said about any White House influence."

"Did you have a chance to talk to Herman and his sister?"

"Yes. She told me she'd heard about the kidnapping while she and her husband were in Washington, D.C. She said she couldn't believe the 'Herman Morales' involved was really her brother, Hermano, until she saw pictures of him."

"So, they're taking Herman to live with them?"

"Well, they have a ranch in Wyoming and they divide their time between there and other homes around the country. Rita's husband said he has a job for Herman on the ranch. That's where he'll be living. Herman couldn't stop smiling, he was so happy. It was wonderful, seeing how devoted he and Rita are to each other."

Gordon's arms closed around her. "It looks like this ordeal has ended happily for everyone involved—except for Herman's partners in crime, back in prison with extended sentences."

"And except for poor Yolanda with her spray-painted van," Deirdre said with a sigh.

Candy was calling them from the dining room. When they all took their places at the beautifully appointed table, they joined hands and asked a blessing on the food they were about to eat.

"And thanks, God, for letting me be here to share this meal with the two people I love best," Candy added.

Gordon was into his second slice of apple pie when Yolanda phoned. Deirdre, who took the call, could tell she was pleased about something.

"What's happened, Yolanda?"

"Dee Dee—the cops all chipped in—they took up a collection for us to get the van painted! The police chief said those bums would never have been found so quickly if it hadn't been for Lupe and his Santo Domingo posse."

"That does it," Candy said, when Deirdre told them. "Everything has fallen neatly into place. What a day this has been!"

After they'd cleared the table and taken care

of the dishes, Candy said she was going to her room to write some thank-you notes.

Deirdre couldn't suppress a smile. She knew Candy had already answered all the notes and cards she'd received from caring people.

"Candy wants us to have some time alone," she told Gordon.

"She knows it's long overdue," he said. "We've had things on hold. . . ." He glanced across the room to where the spiral staircase wound up to the observatory.

"There's a moon tonight. It's almost full," he said.

She knew what he meant. He wanted them to stand, holding hands, in the place where he'd first told her he loved her. And he wanted to tell her again while they watched the moonlight glancing over the treetops.

They climbed the stair, and he took her into his arms and kissed her.

"I'm an old-fashioned kind of guy," he said. "When I told you I was in love with you, I wanted to say something else too, but I knew you weren't ready to hear it. I can say it now. I want you to be my wife, Deirdre."

She looked into his eyes. There was just enough moon to light the look she'd seen there so many times—the look she'd come to know and love.

"I want you to be my husband, Gordon."

Being held in his arms, being kissed again in this, their special place, was a kind of heaven.

"When I said I was old-fashioned, I meant it," he was saying. A moment later he'd taken a small box out of his pocket and was slipping a ring onto her finger.

The moonlight caught the facets of the diamond, sending tiny rainbows dancing in its depths. She wondered if she could ever be any happier than she was at that moment.

"This was my grandmother's engagement ring," he said. "When I called my folks to tell them about you, my mother said she'd send it out to me. She said it sounded like I'd be needing it."

"It's a beautiful ring, darling, and knowing it belonged to your grandmother makes it all the more special." She paused to kiss him before looking at him in puzzlement. "But when did you call your folks?"

"It was right after we were up here in the observatory, before."

She looked at the ring again, smiling.

"Let's call your family tonight."

"We will, but first I have a few things to discuss with you. For one, you know I have more than two years to go before I start my practice. But after the first year is over, in June, the schedule will ease up a bit and I'll be getting more pay. What would you say to getting married in June, dearest?"

She'd marry him tomorrow, gruelling schedule, low pay, and all, if he wanted her to! Aloud, she told him June sounded like an ideal time.

His arms tightened around her. "I shouldn't have let you say yes until I'd warned you. There'll be nights when I'll be on call and I'll have to be near the hospital. It makes sense for me to hang onto my apartment and spend those nights there."

"No problem," she said. "I'll go with you to your apartment when you're on call."

He cast her a grin. "That's some turnaround from what I used to hear from you!"

"Love is a powerful turnaround," she said. "Besides, we both know Candy wouldn't have it any other way."

His face suddenly sobered. "Darling, I know you love this house and so do I, but it's going to be a while before I'll be financially able to take it over."

She could not hold back her laughter.

"My, Dr. Burns, but you *are* behind the times! After you get your practice going, we'll split things, fifty-fifty."

Seeing the doubt in his eyes, she laughed again.

"Come on, let's go down and call your folks. I promise not to embarrass you by telling them what a wonderful, old-fashioned darling you are!"

Chapter Twelve

Candy's surgery was performed the next week. She came home from the hospital the next day.

"I certainly hope this is it," she told Deirdre. "I want to look gorgeous for your wedding."

She'd been ecstatic when Gordon and Deirdre told her about their engagement. Now she was happily making plans.

"After the ceremony we'll have a reception here. The gardens will be beautiful in June, and we can have tables set up around the pool," she said at breakfast a few days later. "There'll be Gordon's family and Grandpa and Grandmother and Aunt Elizabeth, and we'll invite all our friends and Gordon's and Mr. Gillespie and his wife and Ralph. Is there anyone else you can think of, Dee Dee?"

"No," Deirdre replied. She'd been in a delightful daze ever since Gordon had placed the ring on her finger, and had gladly turned the planning over to Candy.

"It's a good thing I'm around to run things," Candy told her. "You're so in love, you're utterly useless. I don't see how you manage to function in the shop."

"In spite of what you think about my state of mind, I'm managing just fine in the shop," Deirdre said. "Except, of course, when Gordon drops in!"

By Thanksgiving, the results of Candy's operation were evident. The scars which had marred her face were fading; her cheeks were smoothing and her nose now looked much the same as before the accident.

"She's going to be pretty again," Deirdre said to Gordon. "We have so much to be thankful for this year."

"Speaking personally, I'm thankful more than ever before," he replied. "For one thing, I've found the woman I want to spend the rest of my life with and, wonder of wonders, she loves me too!"

It was Thanksgiving morning. Gordon had the day off, the shop was closed, and they were in the kitchen, getting the turkey ready for the oven. As usual, Candy had found something very important to do and had left them alone.

In between hugs and kisses, they managed to stuff the huge bird and get it into the roasting pan.

"I never took so long to get a turkey ready," Deirdre said.

"That's because you never had such efficient help before," Gordon replied. He gave her another kiss, then lifted the pan into the oven.

Yolanda had baked pumpkin and mince pies and made creamed onions the day before. Candy's sweet potato and marshmallow casserole was ready for baking and Deirdre's green beans with chestnuts were waiting to be cooked.

Deirdre had invited Jake and Amy and their children for dinner. They were expected later, after Jake was off duty.

"Don't be surprised if Amy brings something to add to this already sumptuous repast," Gordon said.

He was right. Amy arrived bearing a batch of miniature corn muffins, still warm from the oven.

"From an old family recipe handed down from the Pilgrims," she said with a laugh.

They settled the two little boys in the den to watch a favorite show on television.

"With a little luck, that'll buy us about fifteen minutes of adult conversation," Jake said.

"Perfect timing," Candy replied. "By that time, dinner will be ready."

How nice it was to have friends join them this year, Deirdre thought. She and Candy had spent the past two Thanksgivings so quietly. Now she was enjoying the banter and the laughter and the teasing.

"We had to put Gordon on an easy schedule till he got his feet on the ground again," Jake said. "Since I'm going to be best man at the wedding, I felt it my duty to see that he comes down to earth gently."

"I know what you mean," Candy replied, "I don't trust Dee Dee in the shop. She's still way up there on cloud nine."

"I like it up here," Deirdre said. "I may never come down!"

Gordon was sitting beside her on the couch. Hearing her words, he brought her close to him and smiled into her eyes.

"I'm going to make sure you never do come down!"

The day after Thanksgiving had always been especially busy in Old Town. Deirdre and Candy opened the shop early and braced themselves for an invasion of Christmas shoppers.

From the time they opened until early afternoon, the shop had been filled with people, and business had been so brisk that neither of them had a chance to eat lunch. Shortly before two, there was a lull and Deirdre breathed a sigh of relief.

"Much as I like raking in the money, I'm glad the traffic's tapering off. You eat now, Candy— I'll take care of any stragglers and have my lunch later."

"Okay," Candy said. "My mouth has been watering for that leftover-turkey sandwich." She wheeled into the back room.

Deirdre sat down behind the counter and kicked off her shoes. She hoped no one would come into the shop for a little while. It was good to relax and catch her breath and think about yesterday. It had been such fun. It was wonderful to be in love and be loved in return by a man she could trust.

The sound of the shop door opening intruded on her thoughts. She looked up to see Paul. He saw her behind the counter and approached, smiling, flashing those white, even teeth she'd once admired as part of his overall handsome appearance.

"Hello, Dee."

"Hello, Paul. I take it you're doing some early Christmas shopping. What can I show you?"

"Come off it, Dee—I'm not here to shop and you know it."

She wanted to pick up the Acoma pot on the counter and smash it over his head. She managed to squelch her annoyance.

"What are you here for then?"

He walked over to a bench on the other side of the shop, sat down, and motioned for her to join him. When she didn't, he called to her.

"I wanted to tell you I'm glad Candy's all right. That was some surprise, wasn't it—being brought back by the kidnapper himself? It's been the talk of Albuquerque."

"Thanks for your concern, Paul. I'll tell Candy."

"Come on over here and sit with me, Dee. I'm curious about Candy. I heard she isn't going to have surgery—is that true? Will she be in a wheelchair the rest of her life?"

Deirdre glanced apprehensively at the closed door to the back room. She didn't want Candy to hear any of this. Reluctantly, she went to the bench and sat down.

"I can tell by your face, it's true," he said. "Your sister's never going to walk again." He cast her a probing look and added, "Is your cowboy still hanging around?"

It was clear he still didn't know anything about Gordon. If an announcement of their engagement had appeared in the newspaper, he might have more information, but she and Gordon had agreed that a formal announcement might add to the publicity which had surrounded Deirdre and Candy since the kidnapping. Instead, they had let family and friends know by phone and note.

"Paul, it's none of your business whom I'm seeing," she said. Nor was it any of his business what Gordon did for a living, she thought.

He leaned toward her. "Let me give you a word of warning, Dee. With Candy permanently crippled and on medication, nothing's going to come of your so-called romance with that cowboy. He's not going to want to spend the rest of his life saddled with your disabled sister any more than I did. You'll see. Sooner or later, he's going to tell you exactly what I told you—that she should be put in a nursing home."

The door to the back room had opened and Candy was wheeling out. There was no expression on her face to indicate how much of Paul's harsh statement she'd heard. Fervently, Deirdre hoped she'd heard nothing.

"Hi, Paul," Candy said. "It looks like you need to get things straight about Dee Dee's fiancé. He's not a cowboy, but he's in another interesting line of work. He's a resident physician at the university hospital."

Deirdre felt sick at the realization that Candy must have heard every word.

Paul's face betrayed his surprise. It took him a moment to recover, and when he did, Deirdre saw his eyes fill with spite.

"So, you hooked yourself a doctor, Dee? Congratulations. I guess the setup looked as good to him as it did to me. But if you think there's going to be anything different, think again. Doctor or not, he's not going to put up with a paraplegic sister-in-law around the house. Before those wedding bells ring, you'll have to make a choice, just like you did with me."

With that, he stormed out of the shop.

Deirdre turned to Candy and tried to speak lightly to mask her anger and pain.

"I don't know how I could have imagined I was in love with that impossible man."

"I'm the reason you didn't marry him, isn't that right, Dee Dee?"

All Deirdre could do was nod her head. The secret she'd kept so long was now revealed in all its cruelty. How devastated Candy must feel.

"He wanted to shut me away somewhere and you wouldn't go for it," Candy was saying. "I understand now why he suddenly reappeared. Someone told him I was going to have surgery and would be able to walk again. He thought I wouldn't be an annoyance anymore and that I might even get married and go away to live somewhere else. He thought he'd have it made, living here off of your money and not having to take care of your disabled sister."

To Deirdre's surprise, a playful smile had suddenly appeared on Candy's face.

"I take full credit for getting rid of that jerk," Candy said. "If it hadn't been for me, you'd have married him. And then you wouldn't have been free to fall in love with Gordon."

"Oh, Candy...." Deirdre hastened to her side and hugged her.

"Does Gordon know what happened with you and Paul?" Candy asked.

"He knows there was something, but I didn't tell him the whole story."

"Aren't you going to tell him?"

"No. I don't think I want him to know the reason I kept putting him off. I don't know how he might react, knowing I was afraid to fall in love again because of Paul."

"You have to go with your instincts," Candy said. She smiled, patting Deirdre's hand. "I've been doing some heavy thinking. After you and Gordon are married, I'm going to leave you alone as much as I can. After the wedding I'm going back to Florida with Grandpa and Grandmother and stay with them for a few weeks. And now

that dogs don't bark at the sight of my face anymore, and cats don't arch their backs and hiss,
I'd like to take other trips from time to time."

"If you want to travel and the doctors say it's
okay, that's fine," Deirdre replied. "But don't
ever think you'd be an intrusion in our life. This
is your home and always will be. I know Gordon
feels the same way about it."

Candy glanced at her immobile legs. "I know
you mean that, Dee Dee. You've proved it. But
sometimes I feel like such a drag. I wouldn't be
as much of a burden on you if it were only the
seizures, but being unable to walk...."

Deirdre's thoughts went back to the vow she'd
made after her breakup with Paul. Her resolve
was as strong now as it had been then, and she
spoke it aloud.

"As long as I'm able, we'll be together, Candy.
Nothing, no one, is going to put us apart."

On the afternoon of Christmas Eve, Deirdre
and Gordon put the luminarias along the front
of the house and on both sides of the driveway
out to the road. When darkness fell, they lit each
one.

Gordon wasn't familiar with the Southwestern custom of placing candles in brown paper
sacks filled with sand. The candlelight glowed
like gold through the sacks.

Deirdre told him the story behind it.

"To follow tradition, luminarias should be lighted only on Christmas Eve. They're placed outside homes, along walks and drives, to light the way for the spirit of the Christ child."

"The more I learn about the customs of the Southwest, the better I like living here," Gordon said. "I think I'm being transformed into a real New Mexican."

They stood for a few minutes, admiring the spectacle of the luminarias. The air had turned cold with the darkness, and gray clouds now hung beneath the stars. It was the kind of night Native Americans said smelled like snow.

"You could experience your first New Mexico snowfall tonight," Deirdre told him.

"Great—as long as I don't get snowed in up here. I have to be back at the hospital before midnight."

He slipped his arm around her waist as they turned to enter the house.

"If it starts to snow, I'd like to watch it from the observatory," he said.

Inside, Candy was placing some packages under the Christmas tree they'd put up and decorated a few nights before—a tall spruce, freshly cut from from the valley and hauled up to the house by Yolanda's husband Lupe.

"Dinner's ready," Candy said. "We'll eat first, then unwrap the presents."

"Is that another New Mexico custom?" Gordon asked. "Back East, we used to open one present each on Christmas Eve and the rest the next day."

"It's more like a family custom in this house," Deirdre explained. "When we were kids, Candy and I got so excited about Christmas, our parents couldn't resist letting us open most of our presents on Christmas Eve—all except the big ones Santa Claus left during the night."

Gordon looked at her and smiled. "On future holidays, I hope there'll be a couple of excited little kids in this house again."

She knew he had only to look into her eyes to see his hopes reflected.

They ate dinner and unwrapped the gifts. The room rang with laughter when they discovered that Gordon had given Deirdre and Candy each a sweater and Candy had given Gordon a sweater. They all put them on and admired one another, Candy in white embroidered with blue morning glories, Deirdre in tan embroidered with red poppies, and Gordon in blue-and-red argyle.

Deirdre's gift to Gordon was a Navajo silver and turquoise belt buckle.

"Another step towards making you into a true Southwesterner," she told him.

It was Candy who first heard the brush of wind-driven snow against the window panes. When Gordon pulled back the drapes, in the glow of the luminarias they saw a world turned white.

"I'd better get going before it gets too deep," Gordon said.

Candy switched on the television and said, "Let's try to get a weather report. This might not amount to anything."

A bulletin was just coming on, announcing that a sudden storm had hit the Sandias. Heavy snow, combined with high winds, had already caused drifting on the highway east of Albuquerque. Motorists were warned not to travel in the area.

"It can't be that bad yet," Gordon said. "I'm sure I can make it if I leave right away."

Candy shook her head. "This isn't one of your pip-squeak New York snows. When the Weather Bureau out here says stay off the road, you'd better listen."

"She's right, Gordon," Deirdre added. "It can be dangerous driving through the pass in weather like this. You could wind up in a drift. Your car could be buried in snow. I don't want to marry Frosty the Snowman!"

"Did you hear that?" Gordon asked Candy. "She's threatening me!" He looked at his watch and said he'd better call the hospital before all the telephone lines were downed.

"Don't joke about it," Deirdre said. "It *has* happened."

She was glad they were snowed in. That meant she'd see Gordon the first thing in the morning—have breakfast with him, maybe even lunch if the roads were still blocked.

While Gordon phoned the hospital, Deirdre and Candy made up the guest room for him. They all watched *It's a Wonderful Life* on television, and then Candy said she was going to bed.

When Deirdre came back to the living room after helping Candy, Gordon was standing at the foot of the stairway leading up to the observatory. She remembered he'd told her he wanted to watch the snowfall from up there.

They climbed the stair and stood in the place where he'd first told her he loved her and where he'd given her his grandmother's engagement diamond. They watched swirling flakes falling onto tossing treetops and listened to the wind roaring down the slopes.

"This is quite a storm," Gordon said. "Have you and Candy been alone here often when it's like this?"

"A few times. But somebody always digs us out in a day or so."

"How would Candy manage if she were here alone?"

"She'd have a rough time with some things, like bathing and getting to bed. If I'm in the shop and it starts to snow, I close up right away to make sure I can get back home to her."

"You've been a devoted sister, Deirdre."

"I haven't done any more than any sister would do."

"Yes, you have. You've kept Candy with you. It's not easy, being responsible for someone so disabled. Most sisters would have made other arrangements—especially if they were planning to be married."

He took her hands in his.

"Deirdre, I have something on my mind. It concerns Candy."

A sickening fear gripped her heart. She remembered another night and another voice speaking words which sounded much the same.

She looked out into the mysterious whiteness, feeling her spirits fall like the snowflakes into the cold and the night.

"What *about* Candy?" she managed to whisper, although she dreaded hearing the answer that would tell her that Gordon was no different from Paul. Here in this place that was so special to them, he was going to say he wanted to put Candy in a nursing home.

She felt as though her heart were drowning in unshed tears.

"Sweetheart, you're trembling," he said. "Is it too cold for you up here? Maybe we'd better go downstairs."

"No, Gordon—I'd like to hear what's on your mind."

"All right." He started to take her into his arms but she drew away, waiting to hear the killing words and to feel her love wither and die.

She sensed his puzzlement. Always before, she'd gone willingly, joyfully, into his arms.

"I hope you'll consider what I'm about to say very carefully, and if you agree, we can tell Candy tomorrow," he said. "I just learned about a new surgical procedure that has been successful in cases like hers. A few patients regained total use of their legs; others are able to get around with braces. I'm sure Candy's doctor would agree she'd be a good candidate for this operation. But whatever the outcome, I could keep a close eye on her afterward and be alert for any future recommendations, especially after we're married and I'm living in the same house with her—What's wrong, sweetheart?"

In the closeness of their hearts and minds, she knew he'd sensed she wasn't feeling the pure joy his words were meant to bring her. But only she could know her happiness was tinged with guilt for having doubted him.

She reached up and put her arms around his shoulders. She felt his strength encircling her and she knew she could confide it all, at last. She could tell him what had happened with Paul and how, only a moment ago, the old disillusionment had held her fleetingly in its grasp. And he would know it was over and she would never feel the pain again.

"Nothing's wrong, my love," she whispered. "Everything's right."

She had given him her heart. Now she unburdened it, knowing it was safe in his keeping and he would understand.